DUSTY FOG MEETS HIS MATCH...

The small Texan was alerted by the words hissed from the alley behind him, and knew that he had been aiming at the wrong man. He also knew that his assailant, though wounded, was now trapped like a cornered rat, and consequently even more dangerous. There was only one thing to do—shoot to kill.

Todd was dead before he could take aim, his body crumpling sideways like a rag doll.

Dusty glanced over his shoulder. "*Gracias*, Mr. Sangster," he said. "I reckon I owe you my life!"

J.T. Edson

THE CODE OF DUSTY FOG

CHARTER BOOKS, NEW YORK

This Charter book contains the complete
text of the original edition.
It has been completely reset in a typeface
designed for easy reading and was printed
from new film.

THE CODE OF DUSTY FOG

A Charter Book/published by arrangement with
Transworld Publishers, Ltd.

PRINTING HISTORY
Corgi edition published 1988
Charter edition/December 1989

ISBN: 1-55773-288-4

Charter Books are published by The Berkley Publishing Group
200 Madison Avenue, New York, New York 10016.
The name "CHARTER" and the "C" logo are trademarks belonging
to Charter Communications, Inc.

PRINTED IN THE UNITED STATES OF AMERICA

10 9 8 7 6 5 4 3 2 1

For Dorothy Murphy and Charles Mwakai of Kuoni Travel, Nairobi, plus Sammy and all the other safari *bus drivers who have helped to make every visit to Kenya a most pleasant and enjoyable experience.*
Heri na baraka, kwenu-nyote

THE CODE OF DUSTY FOG

Author's Note

While complete in itself, the events in this book follow on from those recorded in: DECISION FOR DUSTY FOG and DIAMONDS, EMERALDS, CARDS AND COLTS.

We wish to thank Dudley Pope—official biographer for Captain Lord Nicholas Ramage, R.N.—for allowing us to borrow the family archives from which we obtained details of the participation of His Lordship's grandson, Sir John Uglow Ramage.

When supplying us with the information from which we produce our books, one of the strictest rules imposed upon us by the present day members of what we call the "Hardin, Fog and Blaze" clan and the "Counter" family is that we *never* under any circumstances disclose their true identities, nor their present locations. Therefore, we are instructed to *always* employ sufficient inconsistencies to ensure neither can happen.

To save our "old hands" repetition, but for the benefit of new readers, we have given information regarding family backgrounds and special qualifications of Captain Dustine Edward Marsden "Dusty" Fog, Mark Counter, the Ysabel Kid and Waco and the points about the Old West about which we have frequently received requests for clarification, in the form of Appendices.

We realize that, in our present "permissive" society, we could use the actual profanities employed by various people in the narrative. However, we do not concede a spurious desire to create "realism" is any excuse to do so.

Lastly, as we refuse to pander to the current "trendy"

usage of the metric system, except when referring to the calibre of certain firearms traditionally measured in milli-metres—i.e. Walther P-38, 9mm—we will continue to employ miles, yards, feet, inches, stones, pounds and ounces, when quoting distances or weights.

J.T. EDSON,
Active Member, Western Writers of America,
MELTON MOWBRAY,
Leics.,
England.

CHAPTER ONE

I *Know* What *They* Say About Him!

"Damn it, Rocky!" Michael 'Mean Mick Meach' Meacher hissed, his accent showing he had been born of none too affluent circumstances in Illinois. "That *can't* be *him*!"

"It *can't*, huh?" Ronald 'Rocky' Todd declared vehemently, never having taken kindly to implications that he might be wrong in anything he said or did. His voice was indicative of similar origins, albeit from a background offering the opportunity of a somewhat better education. "Well it *is* him!"

"He sure as shitting don't *look* it, for all he's wearing a badge!" asserted William 'Bad Bill' Hamilton. He too clearly hailed from the 'Prairie State,' but his tones had a slight Scottish burr and, like his companions, he had adopted a sobriquet which he considered had a tougher sound than his given name. Sharing Meacher's misgivings, he was annoyed by the previous speaker having assumed the mantle of leadership throughout the negotiations which had brought them to their present position. "God damn it! The way those beefhead sons-of-bitches talk about hi—!"

"I *know* what *they* say!" Todd growled. The intonation he gave to, '*they*', indicated he had a similar aversion where Texans—whose dependence upon the cattle business for maintaining the economy of their State had produced the derogatory sobriquet, 'beefheads'[1]—were concerned. "But that

---

1. *How Texans used the vast numbers of longhorn cattle roaming the range country to recover economic stability after the War Between the States is recorded in:* GOODNIGHT'S DREAM, FROM HIDE AND HORN *and* SET TEXAS BACK ON HER FEET.

Will Little jasper's hired m—*us*—pointed him out to me not long after we got here and that's *him* coming!"

There was more than a similarity in the accents of the speakers. All were tallish, fairly well built and had reasonably good looking faces with lines suggestive of vicious natures. A few years earlier, men such as them had formed the nucleus of the gangs of Northern guerillas led by the likes of James "Redleg" Lane. While preaching adherence to the Union, they were just as brutal and unscrupulous as their counterparts riding with William Clarke Quantrell in an equally spurious pretence of serving the South. Deprived of this way of getting money, without the need to raise sweat doing honest work, they had drifted to the West and, as such an occupation was no longer lucrative in their home State, they sought to earn a living by hiring out their guns.

Of the three, Todd presented what some people might have considered the most striking appearance. Having a slight advantage in height over his companions, he had clearly based his appearance upon that of a man from Illinois who had acquired quite an impressive name throughout the West. Not only had he allowed his mousey brown hair to grow shoulder long, but he had cultivated a drooping moustache which did little to improve his features. He wore a flat topped, wide brimmed grey hat with a shining leather band decorated by what looked to be silver coins around its crown, a black cutaway coat, frilly bosomed white shirt with a string bow tie, grey trousers and black boots more suitable for walking than riding. The resemblance to James Butler "Wild Bill" Hickok was taken even further. Two Colt Model of 1851 Navy Belt Pistol revolvers were tucked through the scarlet cloth sash about his waist, their walnut handles turned butt forward in the manner preferred by the famous gun fighter.[2]

Compared to their leader, although neither was willing to

2. *James Butler "Wild Bill" Hickok makes "guest appearances in:* Part One, "The Scout," UNDER THE STARS AND BARS *and* Part Six, "Eggars' Try," THE TOWN TAMERS.
2a. *The circumstances of Wild Bill Hickok's death are recorded in:* Part Seven, "Deadwood, August the 2nd, 1876," J.T.'S HUNDREDTH.

confer that status on him, despite knowing he was a relation of a prominent outlaw, the other two were far less flamboyant. Their round topped, wide brimmed hats were not in the style adopted by Texans, nor—being stout "Yankees" at heart— would they have wished this to be the case, but their clothing was much the same as worn by the cowhands who arrived at the railroad towns in Kansas, delivering herds of half wild longhorn cattle to the shipping pens.[3] The gunbelt each wore was of a kind intended to permit the fast withdrawal of the Colt 1860 Army Model revolvers in the twin holsters.

Two nights earlier, the trio had been paying their first visit to a notorious gathering place for outlaws, Honesty John's Tavern, in Brownton. Wanting to acquire the title "killer," they had been delighted to have the opportunity of shooting down two men in front of an audience they considered—although they had never heard the term—to be comprised of their peers. Having learned that the beautiful young woman they had "rescued from the unwanted attentions" of their victims was none other than Belle Starr, they had expected to be eagerly requested to become members of her "gang." However, their feelings of satisfaction were ended by the scant gratitude she had shown and the owner of the Tavern, Jonathan Ambrose Turtle, had ordered them to leave.[4]

Starting to look for somewhere they would be better appreciated, the trio had heard hurrying footsteps and a masculine voice asking to speak with them. Although they hoped he was sent with a belated invitation from Belle Starr to go into full

3. *How a herd of half wild longhorn cattle was driven from Texas to Kansas is described in:* TRAIL BOSS.
4. *Jonathan Ambrose Turtle was a member of a family which was very prominent in the criminal activities of Texas before independence was won from Mexico until the Prohibition era. Information about a previous, current and later head of the family, Coleman "Cole," Rameses "Ram" and Hogan respectively, can be found in:* OLE DEVIL AND THE CAP-LOCKS; *Part Four, "Mr. Colt's Revolving Cylinder Pistol,"* J.T.'S HUN-DREDTH; SET TEXAS BACK ON HER FEET; BEGUINAGE; BEGUINAGE IS DEAD! *and various volumes of the* Alvin Dustine "Cap" Fog *series, particularly,* THE RETURN OF RAPIDO CLINT AND MR. J.G. REEDER.

partnership with her, or—taking into account that Todd was
related to the well known gunslinger and outlaw, David Short
—that Turtle had had a change of heart and was requesting
them to return, they discovered that neither supposition mate-
rialized. Nor had the precaution of being ready to draw their
weapons proved necessary. The man who approached them
had indicated his pacific intentions by keeping his hands extended well clear of his sides. Of indeterminate age, medium
height and build, although his attire was that of a Texan, he
was heavily bearded and had hair much longer than was considered acceptable by cowhands from that State. Glancing
around to make sure they were not overheard, he had introduced himself as "Will Smith." However, regardless of his
style of clothing and somewhat harsh drawl suggesting his
origins were in the West, he had not appeared to know what
was meant when Todd had asked sardonically, "Is that your
summer name?"[5]

Making no response to the implication that he might have
given an alias, the man had asked to be told the trio's names. He
had apologised for such a breach of range country etiquette, but
claimed he was sure he must have heard of them referred to in the
same breath as other such notable gunslingers as Wyatt Earp,
Bat Masterson and Wild Bill Hickok. Delighted by the supposition, it had not occurred to any of them to wonder why somebody who was going out of his way to give such strong
indications that he was Texan would select the first name in
particular, rather than some of those in the same category who
hailed from the Lone Star State. Furthermore, none had thought
to ask where he had gathered such information about them.
Instead, overlooking the fact that hardly anybody outside their
small home town had heard of them, Todd had introduced
himself and his companions by their sobriquets.

Giving the trio no time to think about any of the conflicting

5. *Waldo "Waxahachie" Smith often complained that he was frequently
the victim of a similar disbelief, even if it was not always expressed
openly, when he gave his surname by way of introduction; see:* NO
FINGER ON THE TRIGGER *and the other volumes of the* Waxahachie
Smith *series.*

points, the bearded man had said how he admired the way in which they had dealt with their "latest" victims in Honesty John's Tavern. However, he had made no reference to their rejection when they had offered their services to the lady outlaw and were summarily ejected by the proprietor. Instead, he had asked whether they would be available to handle a chore for him. Being somewhat quicker witted than his companions, Todd had acted as spokesman before either Hamilton or Meacher could respond. Asking how much the pay would be, before offering to discover what was entailed by the prospective employment, the long haired youngster had been as surprised as his companions at the reply. Quoting a sum of one thousand dollars and saying it would be considered justified when the trio learned the identity of their victim, Smith had supplied the name.

Discovering they would be expected to kill a peace officer would have been sufficient of a surprise for the trio. That the victim was the town marshal of nearby Mulrooney was even more so. Regardless of their antipathy towards Texans, which was based upon cultural indoctrination rather than for any genuine reasons, it had come as something of a shock to learn that the man they were to deal with was none other than Captain Dustine Edward Marsden "Dusty" Fog. Despite pretending to reject all they had heard about him, not one of the trio had believed the task would be a sincecure.[6] If the truth had been told, without the need for discussion, all of them had concluded the chore would prove a vastly different proposition to tackling two comparatively old and unsuspecting dudes like their previous, in fact only, victims.

Realizing his companions were experiencing a sense of perturbation similar to his own, Todd had sought to distract attention from it in case it was noticeable. Contriving to sound much more confident than he was feeling, he had sought to impress the potential employer with his "experience" in such situations. Pointing out that the proposed victim had a number of deputies available for protection, some of whom would

6. *The background and special qualifications of Captain Dustine Edward Marsden "Dusty" Fog are given in:* APPENDIX ONE.

almost certainly have to be gunned down to complete the chore, he had claimed he considered a higher rate of pay was necessary to cover this contingency.

The man, claiming Todd's suggestion of another five hundred dollars was a tribute to his astute business sense, had accepted the terms without argument.[7] With the financial side of the deal concluded, he declared it must be terminated with the minimum of delay. Learning the trio had horses, he had said he would meet them at Hampton's Livery Stable in Mulrooney around noon two days later. Asked by Hamilton why he would not be accompanying them, he had alleviated similar suspicions which the other two were feeling by replying that men with their "considerable experience" in such matters would appreciate how ill-advised it would be for them to be seen travelling together. Furthermore, he had other business to attend to in Brownton and would reach the rendezvous by train. Gratified by the complimentary reference to their supposed experience, Todd had stated his concurrence with the arrangement. His manner had implied, regardless of what the other two might think, that he was satisfied and the offer was accepted.

Although Hamilton and Meacher had not troubled to hide their annoyance at the way in which "Smith" regarded Todd as their undisputed leader, or that Todd considered the same to be the case, they had not been granted an opportunity to rectify the misapprehension. Before the point could be raised by his employees, the employer had said that men of their "considerable experience" would be aware that only travelling expenses were provided at this point in the negotiations. Being unsure whether such was the case, but having no desire to let their lack of knowledge become obvious to one who had so much misplaced faith in their non-existent abilities, the trio had agreed and accepted the twenty dollars they were offered without argument.

7. *We realize the description of the negotiations differs from those recorded elsewhere. Unfortunately, space did not permit us to elaborate upon the matter in:* Chapter Seventeen, "I Want To Hire You To Kill A Man," DIAMONDS, EMERALDS, CARDS AND COLTS.

The negotiations had been carried out in the shadows of an alley between two unoccupied buildings, so there were less details available of the bearded man's appearance than would have been seen if they had been out in the open. However, with the deal concluded, Hamilton—possessing the dour nature of the race from which he had his origins—had suggested pointedly it should be sealed with a drink paid for by their employer, as this was always the case under such circumstances.

Accepting the statement with some reluctance, although its maker had wondered whether he had inadvertently stumbled upon the correct routine, the man had taken them to a small and almost empty saloon. While having the drink, they had inadvertently received a clue as to his identity when he had remarked as verification of what he was saying in answer to a comment from Meacher, "or my name's not Will Little." While he had tried to cover up the error, all three had guessed Todd was correct when assuming "Will Smith" to be an alias. What was more, the inadvertently supplied name had given a clue as to why the man wanted to have Dusty Fog killed.

Having brutally murdered a prostitute at a brothel in Mulrooney, a young man called Kenneth Little from the Ozark Mountains' "hill country" of Missouri had been arrested and held in the jailhouse pending his trial. Knowing that he would be sentenced to death if he was brought before a court of law, a number of his kin had sought to set him free. Not only had their efforts ended in failure but, due to the competence of the town marshal and deputies, Kenneth Little and several of his clan had been killed. Therefore, the trio assumed they had been hired by one of the survivors—impelled with the loyalty to family of their "hill billy" kind—to take revenge upon the man responsible for their death. However, they were not given a chance to ascertain whether the supposition was correct. Having paid for one round of drinks, although Hamilton hinted more would be acceptable, the man had said he must go to keep another urgent appointment and had parted company with the trio. They had decided to follow him in the hope of learning what the undisclosed business might be, but by the time they had considered it safe to make the attempt to leave the saloon, he was nowhere in sight.

Meeting their employer at the appointed time and rendez-vous, once again the long haired youngster had received the majority of his attention. Nevertheless, sensing the arrange-ment was resented by the other two and displaying the posses-sion of tact, Will Little had supplied an acceptable excuse for leaving them behind while he took Todd to see their proposed victim. This had been achieved by stressing the necessity of the precaution of attending to the horses to ensure all would be ready, in case there should be the need for a hurried departure. Despite having claimed nothing could go wrong, Hamilton and Meacher had had to concede the latter was advisable. Like Todd; they knew Dusty Fog only by reputation and would need to be familiar with his appearance—impressive as it was credited to be by his fellow Texans—so as to avoid mistakes when the time came.

Returning alone from conducting the examination, Todd had announced that "the bastard" did not look anywhere nearly as tough and big as was asserted by the other "beefhead sons-of-bitches." Then he had described the plan for carrying out the chore he had received from their employer, although he pretended it was his own. Keeping off the streets until nightfall, in a small and cheap saloon well clear of the main business section, they had set off after dark to implement the scheme. Making their way to a street devoted to business premises, all of which were already closed for the day so that the street was deserted, they had waited for their intended victim to make his rounds. Although they had been warned this might not occur until a subsequent evening, it seemed fortune was favouring them.

Regardless of their claim of disbelieving the stories they had heard about the prowess of Dusty Fog, they had just suf-ficient common sense to realize these must have some basis in fact, and had accepted one fact from the beginning. Satisfying though it would be to claim later that they had achieved their purpose in what would pass as a fair fight, they had declined to seek one. Not that any of them would have admitted openly they had no relish for the prospect of such a confrontation. Instead, they told one another he would never dare accept such a challenge no matter who made it and to issue it would result in immediate intervention by his deputies.

Therefore, with an excuse produced which was to their satisfaction, the trio had turned their attention to some other means of attaining their purpose. Without confessing the scheme had come from their employer, apart from admitting the bearded man had told him their intended victim took turnabout with the deputies at making the rounds, Todd had proposed a scheme and they were now waiting to put it into effect. It had not occurred to any of the three that a man who had so recently taken a wife, as rumour claimed to be the case with Dusty Fog, might refrain from following a routine established in his bachelor days. However, circumstances were proving this was not the case. What was more, when he did show up with reasonable clarity, the sight of him provoked comments indicative of disbelief from Hamilton and Meacher.

"We'll do things the way I said," Todd ordered, rather than suggested, being disinclined to confess to his companions that he had been no less surprised on receiving his first view of Dusty Fog. "Give me time to get around the back and down the alley I showed you, then come al—!"

"We *know* what we've got to do!" Hamilton interrupted coldly. "And time's too short for us to be standing here running it by again."

Giving a low grunt and silently promising himself he would instil a more suitable sense of respect for his leadership upon his companions when they had carried out the chore, Todd withdrew and darted as quietly as he could through the gap between the two buildings from which the observation had taken place. Giving him the time which they estimated he would require to reach his destination, still watching the figure approaching at a leisurely stroll interspersed by pauses to ensure the doors of the unlit and deserted looking buildings being passed were locked, Hamilton and Meacher made preparations for the part they were to play in their forthcoming debut into the trade of professional killers.

CHAPTER TWO

They're Going to *Kill* You!

"Not *that* one!" William 'Bad Bill' Hamilton hissed, as his remaining companion took out the right side Colt 1860 Army revolver. Regardless of the disparaging comments he had uttered on numerous occasions since learning the identity of their prospective victim, he was sufficiently impressed by what he had heard earlier to be unwilling to take any unnecessary chances. "Use the other and, with that "n" being in leather, Fog'll see it and won't wonder why your holster's empty."

"Huh huh!" Michael 'Mean Mick Meach' Meacher grunted, trying to avoid showing he was grateful for being reminded of something he had overlooked in the sense of anticipation mingled with apprehension creeping over him. Despite seeing a far less impressive figure than he had expected, he too had no illusions over the danger they would be facing if the approaching peace officer should suspect their purpose before the trap was sprung. Making the transfer and, holding the replacement in his right hand, he cocked its hammer while continuing, "We'll get him *easy*, Willie!"

"That we *will*!" Hamilton breathed. Normally he would have protested at being addressed by the less robust sounding sobriquet of his childhood. Being just as cognizant of the situation as was his companion, and being equally aware of the possible peril involved, he refrained from objecting to being called Willie. Instead, having already armed himself in the same manner, he estimated that there would not quite have been time for Todd to arrive at the appointed position. Wanting to try and carry out the killing himself and gain the credit personally, albeit with a little unavoidable assistance from the man by his side, he went on, "Let's go get it *done!*"

"Sure," Meacher replied, ever willing to be one of the led rather than a leader.

Concealing their gun-filled right hands behind their backs, but ensuring the empty left was in plain view, the two young men stepped from their hiding place. They were ready to take whatever immediate action might prove necessary, but the intended victim did not present them with any apparent problem. Although he glanced briefly their way as they appeared, he continued to stroll forward without reducing or increasing his pace. However, just before he reached the opening from which Todd was to put in an appearance, he looked in the other direction and stepped from the sidewalk to stride quickly at an angle towards the centre of the street. He acted in such a casual seeming fashion, Hamilton and Meacher assumed he did not suspect their intentions but was merely crossing to check on something he had noticed on the other side.

There was considerable justification for the surprise expressed by the two young men when first seeing Captain Dustine Edward Marsden "Dusty" Fog!

Often, in fact, even people of greater perception found difficulty in reconciling the appearance of the town marshal of Mulrooney with the considerable reputation he had acquired during and since the War Between The States!

Even aided by his high heeled tan coloured boots, Dusty was no more than five foot six in height. Neatly trimmed dusty blond hair showed from beneath the wide brim of his black, low crowned, Texas style, J.B. Stetson hat. Not much beyond his early twenties, while moderately good looking, there was nothing particularly eye-catching about his tanned and clean shaven face when it was in repose. The tightly rolled scarlet silk bandana, dark green shirt—with the badge of town marshal pinned to its left breast pocket—and Levi's pants he was wearing had been purchased recently, but he contrived to give them the appearance of being somebody else's cast-offs and they tended to emphasise rather than detract from his small stature. Nor, despite the rig having been produced specially for him by a master craftsman, was he made more impressive by wearing a well designed brown gunbelt with twin bone-handled Colt 1860 Army Model revolvers butt forward for a cross-draw in contoured holsters. Nevertheless, if one took the trouble to look more closely, there was a strength of will and intelligence beyond the norm about his features and, although his garments tended to distract attention from it, his muscular development was that of a Hercules in miniature.

Despite having ceased to be a bachelor only a few days earlier, Dusty was performing a regular patrol of the town. However, this did not imply there was already something going wrong with his marriage to the beautiful Englishwoman, Freddie Woods, who owned the Fair Lady Saloon and was mayor of Mulrooney. The marriage had been contracted mainly to avert the threat of extradition and standing trial for a crime she did not commit—although being brought to a court of law in England was inadvisable under the circumstances of her involvement with the actual killer.[1] Nevertheless, she and Dusty had already developed a liking which went beyond the respect each felt towards the other in a professional capacity. On the other hand, while having strong feelings towards the vows they had taken at the ceremony, they were realists and appreciated their respective ways of life created problems which most young couples joined in the "bonds of holy wedlock" did not face.

Having been responsible to a great extent for the establishment of the town, in company with a group of businessmen she had met shortly after arriving in the United States, Freddie

---

1. *Told in:* DECISION FOR DUSTY FOG.

1a. *Alvin Dustine "Cap" Fog has instructed us to point out that hints at very close relationships between his grandfather, Captain Dustine Edward Marsden "Dusty" Fog and Belle "the Rebel Spy" Boyd, Vivian "Candy Carde" Vanderlyne and Emma Nene in various volumes of the* Floating Outfit *series were exaggerated. We apologise for having created this misconception, but can only blame it upon the suggestions having been made in the information from which the various incidents were described and as a result of our having been unaware of the true state of affairs between Dusty and Lady Winifred Amelia "Freddie Woods" Besgrove-Woodstole when producing the manuscripts.*

was determined to stay in Mulrooney until satisfied it would continue to run in accordance with the ideals she had demanded when becoming the first mayor. Therefore, to her way of thinking, leaving—for even so good a reason as marriage—was not practical, nor in keeping with her strong sense of duty.

Dusty, too, had his commitments. He had only been taken on as Town Marshal as a temporary measure until the man who was to have held the position arrived—which would be any day now. His period of service as the marshal of Mulrooney was almost up. In fact, even though his time was being put to excellent use, he had already stayed longer than anticipated when he brought in a herd for which he was trail boss. He had been engaged, most successfully,[2] in helping Freddie to maintain law and order during the vitally important period of the town starting to carry out its intended function as a shipping point for cattle driven from Texas. However, he was overdue in returning to his various duties as *segundo* of the OD Connected ranch—the brand being a letter "O" to which the vertical side of a "D" was attached—in Rio Hondo County, Texas; along with carrying out such extra tasks as came his way as leader of the owner, his uncle, General Jackson Baines "Ole Devil" Hardin's floating outfit.

Accepting the situation, the newly weds had had the strength of will to follow the only course each knew was open to the other. The marriage had most definitely been consummated, during the night of the wedding and following a celebration which the invited guests at the Fair Lady Saloon would never forget. Nevertheless, they had agreed their nuptials were to remain in the nature of "convenience" until such time as their respective duties would allow them to turn it into something more conventional.

That afternoon, receiving an invitation to be guest of honour at a banquet given by Steven King—an American delegate for the Railroad Commission assembled at Mulrooney to discuss the extension of a spur-line being built northwards to

2. *Told in:* THE TROUBLE BUSTERS, THE MAKING OF A LAWMAN and *THE GENTLE GIANT.*

join an inter-continental line under construction in Canada—
Freddie had been annoyed to find it was in her capacity as
mayor and for herself alone. She had stated King was still
feeling antagonistic towards Dusty and herself because they
had not treated him with the respect he considered he deserved
since his arrival, so had worded it in that fashion as a means
of taking a petty revenge. On her threatening to decline, her
husband had pointed out it was the kind of function to which
even the senior municipal peace officer would not be invited
under normal conditions. Therefore, if she refused to attend
—or demanded he was permitted to accompany her—she
would be playing into the New Englander's hands. What was
more, it would provide an opportunity for the faction amongst
the citizens who were opposed to her, to claim either her absence was an insult to the influential visitor, or she was taking
an unfair advantage of her office by insisting that Dusty came
too. His absence was explained to the other guests by her
saying he was taking the night watch duty with two of his
deputies.

Leaving the Ysabel Kid and Waco at the office, Dusty was
engaged upon what was generally no more than a routine patrol. Checking on the unoccupied business premises, he had
observed the two young men coming from the alley. Studying
their appearance, he had concluded they were not Texans and
might be the sons of local farmers many of whom wore gunbelts. Having contrived to establish good relations with such
young men since taking office, he was not worried by seeing
them. Nor had a decision to avoid meeting them on the sidewalk caused him to cross the street. Noticing somebody behaving as if wishing to avoid detection in an alley at the other
side, he had felt it incumbent upon himself to investigate.
However, he was not permitted to satisfy his curiosity. He had
reached the centre of the street when he saw the pair leaving
the sidewalk and coming on a converging course towards him:

"Look out, Captain Fog!" yelled a voice with the accent of
a well-educated—albeit alarmed—New Englander, coming
from the alley towards which the small Texan had been making. "They're going to *kill* you!"

Hearing the words, a sensation of alarm brought startled

exclamations bursting from Hamilton and Meacher. They realized that their purpose was betrayed by somebody whose presence they had not suspected, but they took what consolation they could from the thought that they were in an excellent state of readiness to deal with the changed situation. Although they had lost the element of complete surprise, each was already holding a weapon in concealment and, therefore, more readily available for use than the holstered Colts of their victim. With that comforting unspoken assumption mutually shared, they started to bring the revolvers from behind their backs.

Until receiving the shouted warning, Dusty had seen nothing to alert him to the true state of affairs. When the pair left the sidewalk and approached, he had studied them with greater care. However, due to the way the moonlight was throwing a shadow down their left sides, he had failed to notice that only the right hand holster of their gunbelts held revolvers and, because he still thought them to be no more than farm boys, he had drawn no conclusions from the way they were keeping their right hands hidden.[3] Nevertheless, he responded to the danger with the kind of speed for which he had already acquired considerable fame.

Before either could turn his weapon forward, Hamilton and Meacher saw the small Texan's hands cross. Despite considering themselves to be sufficiently fast to make them suitable for their sought after employment as hired killers, never having had anybody except themselves and "Rocky" Todd to help form a comparison, neither had any conception of just how swiftly a gun fighter could make a draw. They discovered there was a *vast* difference between their idea of what constituted speed and the kind Dusty Fog was capable of producing.

It was a lesson from which only one of the young men would be able to profit!

Swept from the contoured and carefully designed holsters,

3. *Although the Colt 1860 Army Model revolvers produced for military contracts had a barrel eight inches in length, those designated the "Civilian Pattern" for a market which is self explanatory were shorter by half an inch.*

with the facility offered by their user being completely ambidextrous, the seven and a half inch "Civilian Pattern" barrels
of the Colt 1860 Army revolvers were brought forward at a
pace neither of the young men could come close to matching.[4]
With the hammers drawn back under trained thumbs and the
forefingers entering the triggerguards an instant *after* the muzzles no longer pointed towards his own body,[5] Dusty aimed
them at waist level and by instinctive alignment. For all that,
offering testimony to his skill, they roared in such close unison that the separate detonations could not be distinguished.
Flying as intended, the two .44 calibre round soft lead balls
each found its billet in the man at which it was directed.

Creating an even greater impact than would a conical bullet
of the same dimensions, the globular chunk of lead from the
right hand Colt had the effect for which it was selected. On
being struck and the ball flattening as it pierced flesh and
bone, Hamilton was knocked backwards before he was able to
complete turning his weapon upon the intended victim. Making an involuntary pirouette which took him away from his
companion, with the unfired revolver dropping unheeded from
his hand, he measured his length on the wheel rutted street.
With his heart torn open by the ball, he was dead by the time
he arrived on the ground.

Because of the speed at which the small Texan had drawn
and fired, Meacher was more fortunate and did not receive a
mortal wound. In fact, by chance rather than deliberate aim,
the bullet did no more than carve a furrow through the flesh of
his right shoulder. However, not only was the shock of the
injury sufficiently numbing to make him drop his gun, it also
spun him around. Toppling over backwards, all the air was
jolted from his lungs by his descent upon the rock hard surface
of the street and, while momentarily stunned, he was still
alive.

---

4. *Dusty Fog was to remember the incident and, later in his career, the
memory would save his life; see:* BEGUINAGE.
5. *How serious could be a failure to take such a precaution when drawing
a revolver is described in:* THE FAST GUN.

Having seen his companions emerging before he was at the mouth of the alley and guessing what they intended to do, "Rocky" Todd felt angry. Watching how the attempt to rob him of the credit for killing Dusty Fog turned out, the emotion had changed to a sense of something close to consternation. However, he also realized that he was being offered an opportunity to complete the assignment unaided and take all the acclaim and payment for himself. Hoping his companions were both dead and would be unable to give information about him to the small Texan's deputies, he thrust himself from his place of concealment and began to raise his Navy Colt.

"Behind you!" the unseen informer shouted, before the surviving member of the trio could achieve his purpose. "There's another in the alley!"

Alarm flooded through Todd as he realized that he too was being betrayed by the man across the street. Nevertheless, he believed his chances were better than those of his companions. The small Texan had passed his hiding place while starting to cross the street and was now facing away from him. With that thought in mind, he lined his weapon at Dusty's back. However, he was prevented from firing immediately.

"Drop that *gun!*" the betrayer yelled and lunged from the mouth of the alley to run across the street.

Without waiting to find out whether the approaching man was armed, assuming this must be the case for the intervention to be made in such a fashion, Todd could not resist the impulse to make him the target. Snarling a profanity, he started to change his point of aim. As he was doing so, he realized there was a more pressing and even potentially greater menace closer at hand.

Having failed to hear the third would be attacker putting in an appearance, Dusty might have fallen victim to his gun without the warning. Accepting it as valid, the small Texan started to swing around. In spite of the speed with which he responded, he still owed his life to the indecision caused by the appearance of the man who had once again alerted him to a danger. Seeing what he was doing and concluding he formed a far more immediate peril, Todd reversed the barrel of the revolver which had been turned away. Nor was it far from its previous alignment.

Only Dusty's superb co-ordination of mind and body saved him!

By the time the small Texan had completed his swing around in a crouching posture which made him a lesser target than if he had remained erect, he was ready to take further action. Firing his left and then the right hand Colt twice in rapid succession, he angled the bullets like the spokes of a wheel. Nor did he allow himself to be distracted by lead from the lighter calibred revolver whistling close by his head as his first shot was discharged. This and the second missed, but it was by an ever decreasing margin. The third ball just grazed the left arm of its intended target and the fourth carved a groove which broke a rib before being deflected without entering the chest cavity. Although the wound was not fatal, or even excessively serious, it proved sufficient for Dusty's needs. What was more, it produced an effect he would have considered eminently more suitable under the circumstances in that he was presented with an opportunity of taking a prisoner to question about the reason for the attack.

Confronted by the figure which suddenly seemed much larger than had previously been the case and spurts of red flame as bullets were sent his way, shock numbed Todd's mind after he had fired the shot. Before he could regain some semblance of control, lead was hissing by him with an eerie "splat!" sound he had never before experienced and which he found chillingly disconcerting. The sting of the ball just touching his arm in passing had hardly registered upon his thoughts when the next made a more potent contact. A howl of pain burst from him as he felt the searing burn and the force with which he was struck, glancing though the blow was, sent him in a sprawl against the wall of the building. Letting the Colt drop from his hands, he flopped to sit with his back against the wall of the building and clutched at his bleeding side.

Whimpering in pain, Todd raised his head with the intention of begging for mercy. He was willing to tell all he knew about the man who had hired himself and his now, he suspected, dead companions, laying all the blame for the attempted ambush upon them. However, before he could speak, his attention went to the man whose presence and warnings had brought him to his present far from favourable situation. Something struck a chord in his memory. It had the effect of driving the plan of action he had elected to follow from his mind.

"Y—You *bastard*!" Todd snarled and, forgetting his suffering in the heat of the moment, his left hand grabbed up the revolver released by his right when he was hit the second time. "It was y—!"

CHAPTER THREE

I Owe You My *Life*!

If his third assailant had continued to hold a weapon on going down, being well versed in every aspect of gun fighting, Captain Dustine Edward Marsden "Dusty" Fog would not have let his attention be diverted from that direction. Satisfied his original pair of attackers were rendered *hors de combat*, at least temporarily—although he suspected permanently where one of them was concerned—he concluded there was no pressing need for him to watch them. Nor, having drawn an accurate conclusion about the quality and abilities of his would-be killers, did he anticipate any further trouble from the other one. Therefore, being grateful for the second warning in particular and wondering whether he was correct regarding the identity of the man crossing the street towards him, he had started to turn his head around. He only intended to satisfy his curiosity quickly, but was not granted the opportunity to do so.

Hearing the words spat out by the assailant from the alley to his rear, who he knew he had only wounded and in all probability not too seriously, the small Texan realized he was wrong with the assumption he had drawn. Instead of wasting time in self-recrimination, he reversed the direction of his gaze immediately and fast. At the sight of Ronald "Rocky" Todd lifting the revolver, he drew the conclusion that either he or—considering the second part of the statement—more probably the man whose warning had helped save him from the ambush was to be the target. Without waiting to discover which of them was selected, knowing all too well the kind of cornered-rat courage which could inspire such actions and

20

make even a wounded man dangerous, his response was that of a well trained peace officer. Taking the brief instant necessary to ensure his aim, he fired his right hand Colt 1860 Army Model revolver in the only way he felt was justified under the circumstances; to ensure an instantaneous kill. Caught between the eyes, with the bullet ranging through his brain before bursting out of the back of his skull, Todd was dead before he could complete his declaration much less open fire at his intended target. His body was jolted against the wall and the gun he had snatched up once more left his grasp. Then he crumpled sideways like a rag doll from which the stuffing had been unexpectedly wrenched.

"*Gracias*, Mr. Sangster," Dusty said, his voice that of a well educated Texan, glancing over his shoulder and discovering his summation about the approaching man was correct. With thumb cocking the revolver he had just fired, even though he was confident neither it nor its mate would be needed again to deal with his attackers, he went on with genuine gratitude, "It's real lucky for me that you was on hand. Fact being, I reckon I owe you my *life*!"

The subject of the gratitude was in his late twenties. Nothing in his appearance made him noticeable. In fact, "average" could describe his height, weight, build and features. Bareheaded, his shortish hair was a mousey brown colour and his face was reddened by exposure to more sun than he was used to in his general way of life. He had on a brown three-piece suit of the latest Eastern style, a white shirt, small knotted blue necktie and Hersome gaiter boots, but he did not appear to be armed in any way. Certainly he was not carrying a gun, as might be expected of one who had become involved in such an affair.

Undistinguished though he might look, and lacking what many Westerners would consider the basic principles needed for survival on their side of the Mississippi River, Dusty knew Raymond Sangster was in charge of constructing the spur-line and was in Mulrooney attending the Railroad Commission. The small Texan was also aware that, perhaps because of his comparative youth and unimpressive appearance, his appointment had not met with the approval of at least one of the

American delegates. According to Freddie Fog, when queried about it by Steven King, Harland Todhunter—the financier and engineer behind the project—had stated, in a manner indicating he was not enamoured of the question, that he was entirely satisfied with the arrangement and the matter had been taken no further.

"I wouldn't go so far as to say *that*," the New Englander objected. "You were doing all right without my help."

"Only part of the way," Dusty corrected, lowering the hammer of the left hand Colt to rest on the safety notch between the two uppermost percussion caps of the cylinder. Returning the weapon to its holster on the right side of his gunbelt, but keeping its mate in his grasp, he gestured to William 'Bad Bill' Hamilton and Michael 'Mean Mick Meach' Meacher. "I'd taken out those two yahoos, but I hadn't a notion they'd an *amigo* close by until you yelled."

"I'm only too pleased I was able to be of help," Sangster claimed.

"So am I," Dusty drawled.

As he spoke, the small Texan was not surprised to hear shouts from various points all around and the sound of running footsteps approaching. Even though practically every grown man in the town carried at least one firearm upon his person, particularly after night had fallen, shooting always attracted attention. The area in which the gun fight had taken place would have struck the listeners as suggesting something far more serious than merely cowhands indulged in a not infrequent habit of firing off their revolvers under the impulsion of misguided high spirits. Therefore, he suspected more than just other members of the town marshal's office were hurrying to investigate the cause of the disturbance.

"I wonder what he meant?" Sangster said pensively, pointing at Todd.

"How'd you mean?" Dusty asked.

"When he grabbed up the gun, he was looking at *me* and started to say what I'm sure was meant to be, 'It was *you*!'," the New Englander explained in a worried tone. "Was he blaming *me* for what happened to himself and his friends?"

"He likely meant it was you warning me that got him

shot," Dusty admitted. Deciding the New Englander was feeling conscience stricken over the incident, he offered the explanation which he believed to be correct and which he hoped would ease the sense of guilt. "But don't hold it against yourself that he was killed, Mr. Sangster. Scared hawg-wild and hurting like he was, he wasn't thinking straight and, unless I miss my guess, he was aiming to make wolf bait of you for doing it."

Before the conversation could be continued, or the first of the approaching people came into view, Dusty and Sangster had their attention attracted to the survivor of the ambush. Having recovered his breath and his wits, using some of the former to emit a long groan, Meacher started to sit up. At his first movement, the two young men swung around. Meacher noticed that the intended victim still held a revolver and was lifting the barrel until it pointed with disconcerting steadiness in his direction. With a sensation of horror, he realized the full gravity of the situation. Nor was his alarm reduced by the recollection of how some of the peace officers in the trail end towns of Kansas were reputed to deal with anybody who tried to kill them.

"D—Don't sh—*shoot*, Cap'n Fog!" the would-be hired killer screeched. Wanting to emphasise his complete lack of hostile intentions, he tried to raise his arms. Although the pain created to his injured shoulder prevented him from fully achieving his purpose, he forced himself to thrust the left hurriedly above his head. "I'm hurting *real* bad 'n' like' to die iffen I don't get took to a doctor fast."

"You should have thought something like *that* could happen to you when you decided to try and kill Captain Fog," Sangster pointed out, stepping forward without coming into the potential line of fire should Dusty be compelled to shoot at the wounded man.

"I—It wasn't *my* notion!" Meacher claimed, staring up at the New Englander for a moment. Then, apparently having concluded he had nothing to fear from that direction, he returned his gaze to the small Texan and, as was often the case when under the stress of some emotion, forgetting the more robust sounding nicknames his companions had adopted, he went on hurriedly, "Ron and Will—Th—*They* made me do it!"

By the time the declaration was completed, the first of the people attracted by the shooting came on the scene. Looking them over, the small Texan discovered the majority of them were a cross-section of the permanent and transient population and concluded their presence was impelled by nothing more than morbid curiosity. Although there was no sign of the local doctor, he noticed the undertaker was coming. At the forefront of the crowd, striding out swiftly and giving indications of being ready to cope with whatever situation they might find, were two of his deputies.

"Looks like you've had a lil mite of trouble, Dusty," suggested the slightly shorter of the peace officers, his accent that of a Texan with a lower standard of schoolroom education, as he gestured at the would-be killers with the Winchester Model of 1866 rifle he was carrying.

"I wondered why you picked this part of town to walk," the taller went on in an accusatory fashion, his manner of speech also that of a son of the Lone Star from a similar stratum of society. Before coming to investigate the disturbance, acting upon the instructions he had received since being sworn in, he had supplemented his basically defensive armament with a double barrelled shotgun collected from the rack on the wall of the marshal's office and was also carrying a bull's eye lantern. "You *allus* grab off the fun chores, Dusty, for shame."

"They always say rank has it privileges," the small Texan pointed out and, having been satisfied he would not be needing it to keep the wounded man passive even before his deputies arrived, he holstered his right hand Colt. Eyeing the youngster in a seemingly warning fashion, he continued, "Which *anybody* who says, 'And some are *ranker* than others,' will wind up riding the blister end of a shovel."

Tearing his frightened gaze from Dusty, who no longer struck him as small and insignificant, but in some way now conveyed the impression of being the largest person present, Meacher stared from one to the other of the newly arrived peace officers. Concluding from their appearances that they must be the Ysabel Kid and Waco, thinking of everything he had heard about them, he found their presence added to the alarm he was experiencing about his position. While both looked somewhat younger than the *big* marshal, each had acquired a reputation for extreme loyalty to Dusty Fog and, regardless of the light-hearted remarks passed between them, they would not be inclined to deal gently with anybody involved in an attempt to bushwhack him.

Lean and wiry, particularly in comparison with the other deputy, the Ysabel Kid was close to six foot in height.[1] Tending to give him a sinister demeanour, every item of his clothing was black and, except for his sharp toed boots having low heels more suitable for walking than riding, of the style practically *de rigueur* for a cowhand from Texas. In addition to the rifle, which somehow looked as if it was an extension to his left hand, at the right side of his gunbelt was a Colt Dragoon Model of 1848 revolver hanging with its plain walnut butt forward in a low cavalry-twist draw holster. Nor did this complete his armament. On the left side was sheathed a massive ivory hilted James Black bowie knife. Being so glossy it seemed almost blue in some lights, his hair was black as the wing of a Deep South crow. Indian dark, unless one looked at his curiously coloured red-hazel eyes—which gave a hint of a *vastly* different character—his features were handsome and seemed almost babyishly innocent.

Even though unable to see the eyes, Meacher was not misled by external appearances and felt he was being studied by the Comanche brave which rumour said the Ysabel Kid had been raised to be![2]

Perhaps a couple of inches taller than the black clad Texan, first impressions of the Indian dark face not withstanding, Waco was younger.[3] Blond haired and with an already well developed physique filling out to powerful manhood, his good

1. *Details about the career and family background of the Ysabel Kid are given in:* APPENDIX THREE.
2. *How the Ysabel Kid acquired the training of a warrior is told in:* COMANCHE.
3. Details about the career and background of Waco can be found in: APPENDIX FOUR.

looking face had lines suggestive of a maturity beyond his years. Apart from the addition of a brown and white calfskin vest, having different colours elsewhere and boots with the traditional high heels of a cowhand, his clothing was much the same as that of his fellow peace officers. Despite only being in his late 'teens, he wore his gunbelt and the twin staghorn handled Army Colts in its low-tied fast draw holsters with the easy assurance of one exceptionally skilled in their use. Offering a suggestion of his presence of mind was the lantern as well as the shotgun.

"Keep back there, folks," the Kid said, his pleasant tenor voice polite and yet holding a note of command giving warning he intended to be obeyed. "'Cepting Mr. Jones and any one of you who's a doctor, to 'tend to who-all of these jaspers needs it."

"I'm a doctor," declared a stocky young man Sangster recognized as Brian Farnsworth, the recently qualified medical attendant who Harlan Todhunter had brought from the East to attend to the physical well being of the railroad construction crew on the journey to Canada. Advancing with the undertaker, while the other people came to a halt, he went on, "Can I have some light, please?"

"There now, Lon, I *told* you this ole lamp'd come in handy for *something*," Waco declared, with the air of one who considered a very wise decision on his part had been completely justified.

"Well, what do you reckon about *that*, Dusty?" the Kid inquired, his tone redolent of amazement. "The boy's got something *right* at *last*!"

"Happen you'd said '*as usual*,' it'd been righter," the blond youngster asserted, wondering—not for the first time—when if ever, he would stop being the 'boy' to the companions for whom he would gladly have sacrificed his life and whom he knew would do the same for him. Putting aside the levity with which he always responded to the apparently derisive suggestions his *amigos* frequently made about him, even though he would not have accepted such remarks from anybody else, he removed the cover from the front of the lantern and turned his attention to the medical practitioner. Adopting an attitude which implied he considered himself above such inconsequential things as the Kid's comment, he continued, "Show me where you want her pointing, doc, and she'll be pointed there's steady's you could ask for."

"Why were they trying to kill you, Captain Fog?" Sangster asked, as the doctor went with Waco and the undertaker to where Todd was lying.

"Now *that* is something I'm figuring on finding out," the small Texan declared somberly. "I can't recall ever having seen *any* of them before they jumped me."

"You mean they're perfect *strangers*?" Sangster asked.

"I wouldn't say they were *perfect*, nor even *close* to it," Dusty answered, glancing with disdain at the whimpering survivor. "But, as far as I can see, they're strangers to me. Like I said, I can't call to mind that our trails have ever crossed."

"I've heard that sometimes men look for famous gun fighters like yourself with the intention of trying to kill them and gain their reputation."

"Such does happen. Except the feller mostly comes alone and wants the fight to be passed off as fair and seen by as many folks as possible. None of them would've expected to get a name by gunning me down from what would be all too plainly an ambush and counted as murder, not self defense, so could have wound up stretching hemp."

"These two are *dead*," the doctor announced, having gone to bend over Hamilton while the conversation between the small Texan and the New Englander was taking place.

"Captain Fog had no other choice but to shoot to kill, Doctor Farnsworth," Sangster claimed, before the small Texan could speak. "They were trying to *murder* him."

"*I* wasn't!" Meacher denied, trying to get up. "Oh Lord, I'm hurt *bad* and likely *dying*!"

"Let *me* be the judge of *that*," Farnsworth suggested, sounding far from sympathetic. "Put the light on him, please, deputy."

"What came off here, Dusty?" the Kid inquired, after Waco had complied and the examination was being carried out.

"These two tried to jump me," the small Texan replied,

gesturing to Meacher and the lifeless body of Hamilton. "Would've done it too, 'cept Mr. Sangster yelled what they were up to. After I'd taken them down, the other one came from the alley behind me. I didn't know he was there and, happen Mr. Sangster hadn't seen him and yelled again, he'd've got me."

"It's right lucky you was around, Mr. Sangster," the Kid claimed and there was genuine gratitude in his voice.

"As I told Captain Fog," the New Englander answered. "I'm pleased I was."

"Not that I'm anything except pleased you was," Dusty said, having wondered how his rescuer came to be in the vicinity so fortuitously. "But weren't you invited to the reception at the Railroad House?"

"I was, but I didn't feel up to another huge meal followed by long speeches so soon after all the rest we've had since the Railroad Commission got here, I asked to be excused," Sangster replied. "I had a few things on my mind and decided to take a walk to try to sort them out. Before I realized where I was, I found myself in the alley across the street and saw those three talking in one over here. Then the man on the sidewalk left the others and went back along the alley. It wasn't until I saw them taking out and hiding their left hand guns behind their backs that I guessed something bad was being planned. I'm not armed myself, so I wasn't sure what to do for the best. Then I saw you coming and shouted a warning. I couldn't do *anything* else, not having a gun. However, as I expected, you were able to deal with the two of them."

"Like I said, you saved me from the other *hombre*," Dusty asserted and, concluding from the way the New Englander moved restlessly that his comment was creating embarrassment, he decided to change the subject. "How bad is it, Doc?"

"He won't be trying to use a gun with his right hand for a spell," Farnsworth estimated. "But he'll *live*."

"Well now," the Kid drawled, seeming to the injured man to become even more Comanche-like and menacing. "I'd not be so *sure* about *that*, was I you, Doc."

"Wh—What do you *mean*?" Meacher croaked, his expression showing he had deduced the worst from the quietly spoken words.

"You three yahoos tried to make wolf bait of Dusty," the Kid explained, his tone still mild even though his bearing was anything except that. "Which we're wanting to know why you did it."

"W—We was hired to gun him down," Meacher replied. Then, seeking to acquire exculpation for his part, he considered he should make his companions appear more dangerous than would be the case if he used the names by which he had addressed them while they were growing up together. "'Least-wise *Rocky* Todd 'n' *Bad Bill* Hamilton was. They *made* me come along with 'em."

"I just bet this gent here saw 'em a-twisting your arm something *cruel* to make you do it," the Kid said derisively. "Who-all hired you?"

"He said his name w—!" Meacher began, but gave a gasp as the doctor moved his shoulder and slumped into a faint.

"He'll talk better after I've fixed his wound," Farnsworth remarked. "And I don't have anything with me to do it here."

"We'll tote him down to the jail," Dusty instructed. "Happen that's all right with you, Doc?"

"I'd rather get his blood over things there than in my room," Farnsworth admitted. "So I'll fetch my bag and join you."

"*Bueno*," the small Texan assented. "Lon, rustle up some help to get the bodies to the funeral parlour. When their *amigo's* able to talk, we'll ask where they hail from and whether there's anybody we can notify of what's happened to them."

CHAPTER FOUR

Nowheres Near's *Big* As Cap'n Fog

"Say, Belle honey," drawled the man sitting at one side of the small table, raising his gaze from the ace, king, queen, jack and ten of hearts he had picked up. His deep baritone voice had the timbre of a well educated Texan and his gaze was redolent of amusement as he continued, "Do you speak French?"

"Enough to get by," admitted the other player in the poker game, having dealt the hand. Her accent suggested a similar background, albeit from elsewhere in the South. Although she had not included 'Belle' as part of her name when signing the register at the Railroad House Hotel, "*Miss Marie Counter, Baton Rouge, Louisiana,*" she raised no objections to being addressed by it. "What do you want to know?"

By any standards, each of the speakers was a magnificent example of their respective gender in the Caucasian subdivision of the human race!

This was especially the case with Mark Counter.[1] Six foot three in height, with a tremendous spread to his shoulders and his torso trimming to a slender waist, he tended to stand out in any company. He had hung his wide brimmed white J.B. Stetson hat on a hook by the door on entering the comfortably furnished room at the rear of the hotel's second floor. Doing so displayed that his curly golden blond hair was cut short in the accepted cowhand style. His bronzed features were almost classically handsome, but exuded a rugged force. Despite

1. *Details of Mark Counter's career, family background and association with Belle Starr are given in:* APPENDIX TWO.

weighing over two hundred pounds, he gave no suggestion of being slow or awkward on his feet. Rather he moved with a springiness indicating a potential for considerable speed when required. Having a deputy town marshal's badge on the left breast pocket of his tan coloured shirt, his attire, while functional, was that of a Texas' cattle country fashion plate. It was made of the finest materials and obviously tailored for him. Placed on the sidepiece, his brown *buscadero* gunbelt carried two ivory handled Colt 1860 Army Model revolvers in fast draw holsters and they clearly had seen much use.

In addition to answering to the name she had not included in her registration, "Marie Counter's" appearance suggested she had supplied false information in the register. On bringing Mark to her room, placing her be-ribboned, wide brimmed, flower decorated white straw hat by his Stetson on the hooks, she had removed a realistic wig of curly and plaited blonde locks. Her own hair was brunette and cropped close around her skull. Furthermore, despite having conveyed a suggestion of being a trifle short-sighted downstairs, she put the gold rimmed spectacles she had worn by the gunbelt.

Also in her twenties, "Marie" was five foot eight inches tall. Although her face had slightly more than the modest amount of make-up permissible for a "good" woman, neither this nor the fact that her top lip was swollen a little as if it had suffered an accident of some kind, detracted from the fact that she was very beautiful. She had on a frilly white cotton muslin organdie two-piece outfit designed to be decorous in cut and style. Nevertheless, the tight fit of the blouse tended to draw attention to the firm full swell of an imposing bosom and the way her torso trimmed to a slender waist. This widened to become curvaceous hips and the material of her skirt gave a hint of them joining shapely legs. There were no rings on her hands, implying she was single and, by convention, she should not be entertaining a member of the opposite sex— especially in such a fashion—without a chaperone.

Earning her living as a very successful confidence trickster, Belle Starr—"Marie Counter" being her current summer name—had never been worried about the possibility of flouting accepted conventions. Having spent a most hectic few

days[2], she had considered she had had enough excitement for
the time being and decided to relax in the company of the only
man who had ever gained her affections. Learning he would
soon be returning to Texas had given her an added inducement
to see him. Nor, despite being on opposite sides of the law,
had she been worried over the possibility of causing him embarrassment by doing so. She maintained secret caches of
clothing and other items of disguise in many places throughout
the West and had recently established one at Honesty John's
Tavern. Examining the contents of the two trunks stored there,
she had selected a personality and alias she felt sure would
prevent her true identity being discovered. Dressed and behaving in a fashion suitable for her pose as "Marie Counter," she
had come to Mulrooney by train early that evening. Taking a
room at the Railroad House Hotel and informing the desk
clerk that she was the blond giant's cousin from Baton Rouge,
she had sent a message to the jailhouse asking him to join her
for dinner.

After eating in the hotel's dining room, holding a conversation intended to convince anybody who might be listening of
their supposed relationship, Belle and Mark had felt sure no
suspicions would be aroused when they came to her quarters.
With their hats, his gunbelt, her wig and the unnecessary
spectacles removed, they had embraced more warmly than
they had been able to do on meeting in the lobby. Then, extri-
cating herself from his arms, she had suggested they played
poker. If anybody who had seen the way she behaved downstairs had been present, the suggestion would have seemed out
of character. What was more, in the light of subsequent
events, it appeared Mark was either surprisingly unobservant
or remarkably trusting.

While the blond giant took a seat at the table in the centre
of the room, the lady outlaw fetched an already opened deck
from the top drawer of the sidepiece. Sitting down, she dealt
the cards without either shuffling or offering them for him to
cut. Despite knowing she was conversant with the etiquette of
poker, instead of commenting upon the omission, he picked

2. *Described in:* DIAMONDS, EMERALDS, CARDS AND COLTS.

up his hand. On discovering he received a royal straight flush, he made the remark about the possibility of her speaking French.

"What does *deja vu* mean?" Mark inquired, again studying a hand which practically every poker player would have been delighted to receive.

vu?" Belle repeated and, although she suspected there was no need for the explanation, continued, "It means you think something that's happening to you has happened before. But I can't for the life of me think what *that* might be."

," the blond giant stated. "But do we have to play out the hand?"

"You *might* win," the lady outlaw asserted.

"Or it could wind up in a stand off," Mark pointed out, despite being aware that the odds on having two such high ranking hands dealt pat were astronomical[3].

"Well that would be *fun* too," Belle claimed. "Unless *you're* in a *hurry*."

"I'm in no *hurry*," the blond giant declared with a grin, remembering the last occasion he and the lady outlaw had played poker in such a fashion.[4] "This's my night off watch and I don't have to get to the jailhouse until nine tomorrow morning."

"Then I'll open with my blouse," Belle stated, reaching for the top button of the garment without waiting for her opponent to say whether he wanted to draw cards. Then her tone became irate. "Oh *damn*, who's *that*?"

"I don't know," Mark admitted. Coming to his feet, he walked across the room. One of the facilities supplied by the Railroad House Hotel was a system of speaking tubes which allowed communication between the rooms and the office behind the reception desk. Removing the cork from the brass

3. *What happened in the previous poker game is recorded in: Part One, "The Bounty On Belle Starr's Scalp," TROUBLED RANGE and its "expansion"; CALAMITY, MARK AND BELLE, (published by Charter Books as TEXAS TRIO).*
4. *An explanation of how the value of the hands rank in the game of poker is given in: TWO MILES TO THE BORDER.*

mouthpiece to bring the high pitched whistle to an end, he listened and, stiffening, snapped, "The *hell* you say!"

"What is *it*, honey?" Belle inquired, knowing only something of considerable importance would have elicited the response.

"Somebody's bushwhacked *Dusty*!" Mark replied.

"Oh my god!" the lady outlaw gasped, coming to her feet and her concern was not a pretense. "Is he—?"

"No," the blond giant said, after having listened to the rest of the news which the clerk imparted, and his tone indicated the relief he was feeling. "He's not hurt!"

"Thank god for that!" Belle breathed.

"I'm sorry, honey," Mark apologised, "But I've got to go down to the jailhouse and see if Dusty needs any help."

"Of course," Belle assented without hesitation, despite darting a glance redolent of disappointment at the cards. In addition to knowing it was the blond giant's duty as a deputy to report to the town marshal's office, she also knew of the close bonds of loyalty each member of Ole Devil Hardin's floating outfit felt towards the others, and she had expected that decision to be made. What was more, having the greatest respect and liking for Dusty, she was willing to give any assistance her association with outlaws could produce if it was needed. "And I'm coming with you."

"Now we know who you are 'n' where you're from, which'd best be *right* happen you want to keep a whole hide," the Ysabel Kid said, the information having been given by the prisoner cowering on a chair. He sounded like a Comanche Dog Soldier eager to inflict cruel and painful treatment. "Who hired you to gun Cap'n Fog down?"

Recovering from the faint, Michael Meacher had found himself in what he realized was a cell. While he was receiving treatment, he had had his forebodings increased by hints from the doctor about the fate awaiting him unless he was forthcoming when questioned about the ambush. With the wound bandaged, he was fetched into the main office of the jailhouse by a pair of deputies who he had not seen before. Their attire respectively that of a successful professional gambler and an

Army scout and they looked just as unfriendly and menacing as the Texans who had arrived at the scene of the ambush. Suspecting the worst, when ordered to sit down, he had crouched like a dog expecting to be whipped on the chair placed by the desk.

The posture adopted by the prisoner was not caused by the pain he was suffering. He was so perturbed by the coldly hostile faces of the five men wearing badges who were forming a rough half circle about him that he was barely conscious of the throbbing ache which still came from the bandaged injury. Until that evening, his sole contact with lawmen had been a brief acquaintance with the elderly and far from zealous constable of his home town in Illinois. He realized he was now dealing with far more dangerous and intelligent peace officers who were determined to get the truth from him. With that in mind, instead of saying "Mean Mick Meach," he had given his real name and home town when Dusty Fog had commenced the questioning with a demand to be told who he was and where he came from.

"N—Not m—*me*!" Meacher denied, looking nervously from the intended victim to the Indian dark deputy and back. "It was Roc—!"

"Happen we *believed* you, which we *don't*," Waco interrupted, sounding as coldly threatening as he and all the others were contriving to appear. "Seems to me's you'd've made certain sure's you got to *know* who-all'd done the hiring."

"I—I *didn'*—!" Meacher began, diverting his attention briefly from Dusty to the blond youngster and intending to resume his earlier attempt to convince the obviously sceptical group that he had been an unwilling participant in the ambush.

"The hell you *didn't*!" interrupted Deputy Frank "Derry" Derringer, whose knowledge of gambling had been put to good use since he became a peace officer.[5]

"H—He told Rock—*us*—his name was 'Will Smith!'"

---

5. *Deputy Town Marshal Frank "Derry" Derringer makes appearance in:* QUIET TOWN, THE MAKING OF A LAWMAN, THE TROUBLE BUSTERS, THE GENTLE GIANT and COLD DECK, HOT LEAD.

Meacher declared hurriedly, concluding things would go badly for him unless he supplied what few answers he could.

"*Smith!*" Deputy Albert "Pickles" Barrel snorted, having accepted the post of jailer after his retirement from being a scout for the U.S. Cavalry.[6]

"Th—That's what he *tried* to make us figure he was called," Meacher hastened to elaborate. "But he let on who he really was while he was talking to us."

"Now who'd that be?" the Kid prompted.

"Will Little," Meacher supplied, watching for and failing to see any suggestion that the name was known to his interrogators. "*Little*, like them jaspers you had fuss with a few days back. You've got a couple of them in there."

"We have," the small Texan conceded. "But they haven't mentioned any of their kin being hereabouts. What did this 'Will Little' *hombre* look like?"

"H—He was dressed and talked with a bee—!" Meacher replied and realized the derogatory term would be inadvisable in his present company. "*Texan!*"

"A *Texan*?" the Kid put in disbelievingly. "All the Little's we locked horns with hailed from Missouri."

"He could've tried to sound like a Texan, so's we wouldn't know who he was," Meacher suggested, his face showing fright. "He'd been telling us his name was 'Smith' until he let 'Will Little' slip out."

"Where did you meet this jasper?" Waco demanded.

"On the street in Brownton," the prisoner replied. "He come after us when we'd got run out o—*left* Honesty John's Tavern."

"I'd say you'd got it *right* first time 'bout why you lit a shuck," the Kid asserted, wanting to squash whatever spark of spirit had caused the revision. "They do tell Honesty John's mighty picky about who-all he lets in."

6. *Due to an error in the material from which we first wrote about Albert "Pickles" Barrel, we inadvertently referred to him as "Pickle-Barrel" and implied he had been working as a swamper at the Fair Lady Saloon prior to being hired as jailer. In actual fact, he was already employed in the latter capacity by Freddie Woods before Dusty Fog took over as town marshal.*

"That's for sure," Derringer supported. "Anyways, see-ing's how he wouldn't give it all to knobheads like you afore you'd done your chore, where'd you fix to meet whoever he is to get the rest of your pay?"

"At the Big Bull," Meacher replied, naming the rendez-vous in the hope it would lead to the arrest of the man he blamed for his predicament. "It's down by the—!"

"We *know* where it is," Waco interrupted, then looked at Dusty. "He's likely heard what's come off and lit a shuck by now."

"Could be," the small Texan agreed. "What does he look like?"

"L—Look l—like?" Meacher repeated in a flustered voice.

"Was he good looking or ugly?" Waco inquired.

"I couldn't say for *sure*," Meacher admitted worriedly. "H—He'd got a beard's covered most've his face."

"What colour was it?" the blond youngster asked.

"Brownish," Meacher supplied, after a moment's thought. "Like his hair."

"Most men's beards're the same colour as their hair," the Kid injected dryly. "How tall was he?"

"Tall?" the prisoner gasped.

"*Tall*, god damn it!" the Indian dark Texan thundered, looking at his most savage; which meant he presented a very terrifying aspect to the already frightened young man. "I'm getting quick sick of having to keep on *asking* things's don't get a straight answer!"

Despite the menacing aura exuded by the Kid and the other deputies—all of whom were much taller and, on the surface, more impressive in appearance—Raymond Sangster noticed Meacher appeared most disturbed by the small Texan. In fact, although he repeatedly glanced at whichever speaker was ad-dressing him, his gaze quickly returned to Dusty and was re-dolent of awe. Dangerous as he showed he considered the others must be, it was apparent who he considered posed the greatest threat.

Remarking that Dusty probably wanted to reassure his wife that the ambush had failed, the New Englander had offered to help Waco carry the unconscious prisoner and allow the Kid to go to tell her. On the way to the jailhouse, his belief that the small Texan intended to try and discover who had hired the trio was verified. He had also noticed Doctor Farnsworth had not hesitated before agreeing to help when told how this could be done. Before the plan could be commenced, the Kid had returned accompanied by Derringer and Barrel, each of whom had left what he was doing as soon as he heard the news. Despite being off duty that evening, they had stated their willingness to remain and give assistance in creating the atmosphere which the prisoner had found so alarming and conducive to a desire to answer the questions he was asked.

"Was he as tall as *me*?" Sangster suggested, stepping forward.

"T—Taller," Meacher estimated. After turning his gaze from the small Texan to direct a glance from the New Englander to the Kid, he continued, "He wasn't nowheres near as *big* as Cap'n Fog. But about 'tween you and the deputy there."

"Was he fat, or thin?" Sangster continued, having found the estimation of the heights very significant despite its inaccuracy and being able to appreciate what had caused the prisoner to make the mistake.

The supposition with regards to the reaction of the prisoner to Dusty's size strengthened the New Englander's belief that he was correct in the assessment of the small Texan's character. Ever since he had become aware of Dusty's full potential, he had wished that he could win a similar respect and exert such dominance over men from many walks of life. Being endowed with the ability to exude so great a strength of personality that it transcended mere physical appearance would be of the greatest assistance to him in the work upon which he was at present engaged.

"Not thin," Meacher asserted after a moment's thought, although he still had only the vaguest recollection, but he hoped to avoid the painful treatment he was expecting to receive if he failed to supply satisfactory answers. "I'd say he was hefty."

"None of which helps us much," Dusty remarked, concluding the prisoner could not say anything else which would be of use. "If he was one of the Little family looking for evens, he could've been wearing a disguise. This *hombre* wouldn't've noticed it wasn't a real beard and I don't reckon the two yahoos who were with him would be a whole heap smarter. Put him back in the women's cell for now and maybe he'll come up with something else later."

"There *might* be a way you could find out whether the Little family's involved," Sangster said, after Meacher was taken from the office by Barrel. His tone was deferential and indicated eagerness to help. "If you don't mind a suggestion, that is."

"I'm *always* willing to listen to suggestions," Dusty claimed, then threw a mock derisive look at his deputies. "Depending on who-all makes them."

"I was always keen on amateur theatricals while I was at college and might be able to pull it off," the New Englander concluded, having explained his idea. "And I've got some clothes that would help down at the hotel."

"Go with Mr. Sangster and lend a hand, boy," the small Texan instructed. "And, while you're at the Railroad House, happen he hasn't already heard, you'd best tell Mark what's happened."

CHAPTER FIVE

Who Did the Hiring?

Crossing the slightly sloping roof of the lean-to where the hotel kept a couple of vehicles that were used for collecting customers' baggage from the railroad depot, Belle Starr was pleased she had been able to obtain a room at the rear overlooking the roof. Dressed as she was, not only had she reached it from her window without difficulty but she could easily descend to the ground and she was confident she would be able to return by the same route when her business was concluded. While the changes made to her appearance might have allowed her to go out through the first floor without any of the other guests suspecting the deception, she had felt sure the same would not apply to Mark Counter and Waco if they were still in the lobby.

Meeting the youngster when she and the blond giant had come downstairs caused the lady outlaw to revise her plans. He had explained that he was waiting for Raymond Sangster, who had gone to his room to make the preparations required for a plan to discover whether a member of the Little family was responsible for the attempt to kill Dusty Fog. Asked for further information about the abortive ambush, Waco's comments on the unsuitability of the trio for the task had included a scathing reference to the one dressed like Wild Bill Hickok. Remembering her thoughts when she had seen the man who, the prisoner claimed, had hired them watching and following them from Honesty John's Tavern, she had decided to conduct an investigation in the hope of discovering, if not his identity, something to help track him down. Deciding not to mention certain suspicions she had drawn about the mysterious employer, she had excused herself from accompanying the Texans to the jailhouse on the grounds that the survivor might recognize her. Then she had returned to her quarters.

On her arrival in Mulrooney, Belle had only intended to relax in Mark's company. Nevertheless, being aware that she led a most precarious life as a result of her various illicit activities, she had taken the precaution of packing clothing other than that suitable for wear by her *alter ego* in the trunk which was her only piece of baggage. Wanting to be less noticeable on the streets than would be possible as "Miss Marie Counter," she had chosen from the masculine attire which was included. The selection consisted of a flat cap and a brown two-piece suit—with the jacket sufficiently baggy to conceal her more obvious feminine physical attributes and the Manhattan Navy revolver tucked into the waistband of her trousers—a white masculine shirt and dark blue necktie. To complete the ensemble, she retained the black riding boots concealed by the long skirt when wearing her feminine attire. Dressed in such a fashion, which offered a greater freedom of movement than her female raiment, she felt sure she could pass in the darkness as a male visitor from the East and would be unlikely to attract attention while going to her destination.

Reaching the ground without hearing anything to suggest her unorthodox way of leaving had been observed, the lady outlaw strode swiftly away. Continuing at a brisk walk, she was soon on the fringes of the middle class area and arrived at her destination. Standing in the centre of a small garden, with glints of light showing from small gaps in the drawn drapes to suggest the occupants had not retired for the night, the house looked no better nor worse than its neighbours. However, opening the gate in the picket fence and walking along the path, she felt sure that—if anybody in Mulrooney could—the owner would be most likely to satisfy her curiosity about the attempted killing of Dusty Fog. Knocking on the front door, after a few seconds, she heard footsteps approaching.

"Yes," called a masculine voice with a New York accent. "Who is it, please?"

"*Shalom*, you-all!" the lady outlaw answered just loud enough to be heard. Without needing to see a small circle of light in the middle of the door, she knew she was being studied through a concealed peephole and, feeling sure the observer had not recognized her, gave verbal proof of her identity. "Can I come in, Edmund?"

"Of course, my dear," the voice agreed, the words accompanied by the sound of bolts being drawn and a lock turned. However, on the door being opened, Belle was not surprised to discover the lantern used to examine her through the peephole was placed so it would reveal little of her appearance to anybody who might be watching. "Momma's off playing whist with her lady friends and the boys aren't here, so I'm all alone. Come in and welcome."

Crossing the threshold, with the speaker quickly closing the door, the lady outlaw accompanied him to what looked like the combined sitting-room and office of a not too wealthy businessman. Nevertheless, unimpressive though it might be, she was aware that it served as the centre from which the operations of a network of receivers and information brokers for the criminal element of the West were directed. There was not so much as a hint that it often held large amounts of stolen jewellery, money, and other kinds of easily portable loot, before they were concealed in a hiding place where the speaker took delight in challenging those few privileged illicit customers who came into personal contact with him to find. Although they—and Belle—were experts at locating such places, his secret had never been discovered.

A couple of inches shorter than the lady outlaw, Edmund Fagin was plump and jovial looking. The black skullcap, dark blue smoking jacket, collarless white shirt, yellowish brown Nankeen trousers and old carpet slippers he wore were no more expensive than the attire of his neighbours. In fact, like his surroundings, nothing suggested he carried on a long established family tradition by being the most successful fence in the West and very knowledgeable about criminal matters of all kinds. When anybody with literary leanings commented about his surname, he would laugh depreciatingly and reply,

"My life, *no*. I'm not related in any way to the 'Fagin' that Britisher, Mr. Dickens, wrote a book about."[1]

"Well now, my dear," Fagin said, after having seated Belle in a comfortable chair and poured her a glass of *Mogen David* wine; something he only did for visitors who he held in high esteem. Aware that she knew his way of operating through intermediaries, unless the loot involved was especially valuable and as he had not heard of her acquiring such, he went on, "Have you something of a particular interest to *me*?"

"There are some quite good diamonds headed down your pipeline," the lady outlaw answered in an offhand tone. "But they're not why I've come. You've heard what happened to Captain Fog?"

"I have," the fence confirmed and, although Belle felt sure such was not the case, his tone apparently expressed no more than casual interest. "In fact, I've sent the boys to find out all they can. Do *you* know anything?"

"Such as?"

"Were the men who tried it somebody he knew?"

"No. The one who came through it alive claims they were hired for the chore."

"*Hired?*" Fagin repeated, showing puzzlement to somebody who knew him as well as did the lady outlaw. "Do you know them?"

"We met briefly and just the once," Belle admitted. "Even though one said he was kin to Dave Short, I wasn't impressed."

"*Dave Short?*"

"That's what he said, but he might only have been trying to impress Honesty John and me."

"Not if he's who I think he might be, my dear. Word from

---

1. *Although there was no physical resemblance between them, the researches of the world's foremost fictionist genealogist, Philip Jose Farmer—author of, amongst numerous other works,* TARZAN ALIVE, A Definitive Biography Of Lord Greystoke *and* DOC SAVAGE, His Apocalyptic Life—*have established that Edmund Fagin was a grandson of the man about whom Charles Dickens wrote in:* OLIVER TWIST.

Mr. Short's been making the rounds that a young nephew of his and two friends are trying to set up as hired guns and *nobody* is to give them work on those lines, or he'll be coming to ask why."

"He must be real keen to have them stopped getting their wantings."

"You could say that," Fagin answered dryly. "So keen he's said he'll be looking for anybody who either hires them, or even arranges for them to be taken on—and he won't be looking *peaceably*."

"Then who did the hiring?" Belle asked, knowing the man in question to possess sufficient of a reputation as a gun fighter to have his wishes on the matter respected by most people.

"I haven't heard even a hint that anybody wanted to kill Captain Fog," Fagin declared. "Much less was looking to hire it done."

"'Mean Mick Meach,' as he calls himself, was the one to come through it alive," the lady outlaw said, but failed to detect any trace of the name having struck a chord with the fence. "He allows it was one of those Missouri hill country Littles who've been raising fuss around Mulrooney."

"They've cause and we both know how their kind always go for evens," Fagin answered. "But, as far as I know, all of them who were hereabouts got gunned down the night they tried to break their brother out of the jailhouse. There wouldn't have been time for word to get back to the Missouri hill country and some more to come."

"That's how I see it," Belle conceded. "In fact, I'm sure the man I saw follow them, when Honesty John told them to leave his place, is who hired them and, unless I'm mistaken, he was wearing a wig and false beard. There wouldn't be any reason for a disguise if he was one of the Little bunch, at least not at the Tavern."

"So why have you come to me?" Fagin inquired.

"You've already answered that," the lady outlaw replied. "If *anybody* would have heard should somebody have been trying to hire men to go after Dust—Captain Fog, it would be *you*."

"My life!" the fence ejaculated. "You don't think I would have been such a *meshuge*—so *crazy*—I'd even *think* of taking up such a proposition?"

"Not for a moment," Belle asserted placatingly. "But you *would* have heard if anybody else was thinking of it."

"I wish I could help you, my dear," the fence claimed and his sincerity was genuine. "If the ambush had come off— Well, I wouldn't have wanted to even stay in Kansas the way Miss Woods and the rest of the OD Connected crowd, from Ole Devil Hardin to that boy, Waco and—," the next words were accompanied by a genuine shudder indicative of greater alarm, "the Ysabel Kid in particular—would have started hunting for whoever did it. This whole State and the rest of the West would be too hot to live in until they'd found out and taken their revenge. As it is, except to those three young fools who tried to kill him, no harm's been done. All right, so Short's been making threats. I'd bet Captain Fog can deal with *him* once he's heard about them."

"What Dave Short might *try* won't make me lose any sleep, because I'm going to warn Dusty," the lady outlaw asserted, meaning give the information to the small Texan as soon as possible and save Fagin doing so. "It's whoever hired them worries me. He's failed to have it done once, but he's likely to try it again."

"Hey, Mean Mick Meach!"

Seated huddled against the rear wall of the jailhouse on the hard wooden bunk he had selected, holding his still throbbing injured shoulder with the other hand, Michael Meacher looked more like the frightened young man he was than the professional killer he and his two dead companions had aspired to become. What was more, such was his dispirited condition, his brain failed to register hearing his "tough sounding" sobriquet.

Although Meacher had not been subjected to any of the brutality he had expected and feared, the interrogation to which he had been subjected by the peace officers combined with the disastrous results of the attempted ambush, had left him in a condition of self pity and alarm. Nor had he recovered from it while alone in the smaller room in which he had been incarcerated, until the arrival of a big woman wearing the badge of a deputy town marshal, escorting two dishevelled and protesting saloon-girls, caused him to be transferred into the main block of cells. Shortly after being put there, he was given what, in different circumstances, he might have considered company. Waco and the Ysabel Kid had brought in a man whose demeanour implied he had drunk "not wisely but too well" resulting in his arrest. Paying no attention to Meacher, he had flopped on to the other bunk and sung drunkenly while watching his gaolers return to the front of the building and close the connecting door.

"Hey, '*Mean Mick Meach*'!" the newcomer repeated, his harsh Western accent taking on a timbre of urgency.

Slowly Meacher began to appreciate a change had come over the man. Leaning forward on the bunk, all trace of drunkenness had left him. However, despite the urgency in his voice, he was a far from impressive sight. Of medium build, with a straggling mop of longish brown hair and a dirty face marred by a long scar on the left cheek, his attire was the kind often worn by poorer town-dwellers.

"No offence, but I *know* you," the newcomer went on in a placatory and apparently admiring tone. "There's only *one* 'Mean Mick Meach' and it's a real privilege to make your acquaintance. Did them bastard john-laws work you over?"

"No," Meacher admitted and his voice rose as he continued. "But who're y—?"

"Talk *softer*!" the newcomer hissed, nodding to the wooden wall between the cells to warn there were occupants on the other side. "They likely reckoned's they'd be wasting their time to do it. *Everybody* know's how, no matter what those two yahoos you had helping you might've done given they'd been caught 'stead of made wolf bait, Mean Mick Meacher's too staunch to talk no matter what gets done to try and make him."

"And I *was*!" Meacher declared, sitting up straighter under the influence of flattery. As had happened during the meeting with the bearded man in Brownton, he was too delighted by the treatment—which formed a most pleasant change from the way the peace officers had behaved—to question where the newcomer had heard about him. Wondering why the other's voice sounded vaguely familiar, he went on, "Anyways, I don't recollect our trails having crossed. Who're you and why've you come here?"

"I didn't come over and say, 'Howdy, you-all' in Honesty John's after you'd taken down those two jaspers," the man replied, making the words sound like an apology. Rising and stepping forward, holding out his right hand, he did not supply the requested information. Even if he had, he would not have told the truth by admitting he was Raymond Sangster in disguise, putting into effect the plan he had outlined to Dusty Fog. "But it was nice a piece of work as I *ever* clapped eyes on and I've seen *plenty*. Hell, you didn't *need* those other two yahoos to help. You could've tooken them out yourself."

"I *could* have," Meacher boasted, without offering to shake the offered hand. His spirits had risen to a pitch where he overlooked there having been no mention of the way he and his companions had been ordered to leave the Tavern by its owner in a very disrespectful manner considering his supposed importance. Starting to believe he really was "Mean Mick Meach" and had the qualities assigned to him, he adopted a tone of demand as he continued, "But I still haven't heard *your* name!"

"Herbie Smith," Sangster lied, impressed by the way in which the tactics suggested by Dusty Fog were achieving the desired effect. "I'm kin to *Will Smith*."

"*Smith!*" Meacher snorted. "Don't hand me that bullshit, mister. I *know* his name's Will *Little*!"

"Hot damn!" the disguised New Englander ejaculated, slapping the rejected hand against his thigh. "I told Cousin Will's how, no matter he'd fooled those other two, you'd seen through his summer name and knowed who he was."

"There's not *much* gets by *me*," Meacher boasted. "Where's he at?"

"Up to Brownton," Sangster supplied, watching for any suggestion to indicate the young man knew he was lying.

"I figured he would be, seeing's how he come after us from Honesty John's," Meacher claimed. "And, way you acted when they brought you in, you've got something to tell me from him."

"That I have. He says for you to sit back and don't go busting out, 'cause, less'n you've already got one, he'll be getting a lawyer for you."

"I don't have and the son-of-a-bitch's he gets for me'd better be the best 'n' around."

"Only the *best* is good enough for you, Mean Mick," Sangster asserted. "We've got a feller watching the office from across the street, so I'll go signal like we fixed up that you'll need the law-wrangler." Raising his voice, he yelled, "Hey out there!"

"You got it done, huh, Ray?" Dusty Fog said, coming through the connecting door followed by some of his deputies.

"Flattery worked, just like you said it would," Sangster announced, reverting to his normal mode of speech and going to the door of the cell. "He accepted it when I told him the man was Will Little and had gone to Brownton to get him a lawyer, so I'm sure he doesn't know any more about who did hire him than he told you."

"You've done real good, *amigo*," Dusty praised, watching an expression of what he assumed to be horror come over Meacher's face and having no doubt the mood of despondency would soon return now he had received proof of how easily he had been tricked. "Open up and let Ray out, Pickle."

"I won't be sorry to get this wig off and cleaned up," the New Englander stated, on the order being carried out. However, as he and the peace officers were walking away, none noticed the speculative way in which Meacher was studying him. "Wearing a disguise always makes me feel so dirty."

2. *All three women worked for Freddie Fog—as she now was, although she continued to use her adopted maiden name 'Woods' for some time to come—at the Fair Lady Saloon. The largest acted as deputy town marshal when female prisoners required attention and the other two were present to help supply a reason for transferring Michael Meacher to the main cell block so Raymond Sangster's plan could be put into effect.*

CHAPTER SIX

You Look Like a Man With Problems

"Howdy there, Ray," Captain Dustine Edward Marsden 'Dusty' Fog greeted, turning from studying the window display of the gunshop on Trail Street as the New Englander was hurrying past with an air of preoccupation which explained the lack of acknowledgement from him.

"Oh hello, Dusty," Raymond Sangster replied, sounding startled. Jerking his head around and coming to a halt, he went on apologetically, "I didn't notice you."

"It looked that way," the small Texan admitted with a grin, starting to stroll along the boardwalk at the side of the New Englander.

"I see you're not wearing your badge," Sangster remarked.

"Not any more," Dusty confirmed. "Kail Beauregard got in yesterday and I've handed over the office to him."

"So you've not got anything to stop you going home?" the New Englander inquired, a touch of disappointment in his voice.

"Nope," the small Texan replied. "But we won't be lighting a shuck straight off. The boys say they want to have some of the fun they missed through us taking over as peace officers so soon after we got here and that'll let Freddie and me spend a few days together now she's not busy with the Railroad Commission."

It was mid-afternoon three days after the abortive ambush. During that time, Dusty had become satisfied Sangster was correct in claiming Michael Meacher did not know the identity of the man responsible for it. Having received a message from a confederate which caused her to terminate her visit more

49

quickly than she had anticipated, Belle Starr, before leaving, had passed on the information gleaned from Edmund Fagin—without revealing, or being asked, its source—and her belief that the employer of the trio had worn a disguise at Honesty John's Tavern. She had not heard anything more from the fence to suggest the man was seeking replacements to try again. Nor had there been any further attempts to kill the small Texan.

What Sangster achieved with his plan had made the peace officers more inclined to be friendly than might otherwise have been the case, their respective interests and social backgrounds being so dissimilar. Despite the willingness he had shown to help deal with Meacher, even where Dusty was concerned, except for having come on to first name terms, he had made no attempt to keep in closer contact than previously. Going by appearances, he had been too occupied with his duties to spend much time on relaxation. Mostly they had seen him hurrying around in a harassed fashion, attending to whatever matters might be arising in town or from the work already taking place on the spur-line.

"You look like a man with problems," Dusty commented. "Having trouble with the Railroad Commission?"

"No," the New Englander denied, but his voice lacked conviction. "I can leave dealing with *them* to Mr. Todhunter. Up to a point, that is."

"I'd say the 'point's' getting close, or has come," Dusty guessed and, having noticed the emphasis placed upon the word, 'them,' continued, "Are you having some kind of trouble with the construction work?"

"N—Well—*Yes*, I am. But I don't want to saddle you with *my* problems."

"My daddy always told me a trouble shared's a trouble halved."

"But—!"

"If it's something private and confidential—!"

"It's nothing like *that*, Dusty. Well, not in the sense you mean."

"Then let's go in the Fair Lady and talk about it."

"Very well," Sangster assented, the saloon having been

reached while the conversation was taking place.

Entering the elegantly furnished building and glancing around the main room, the New Englander was pleased to find neither the owner nor any of the floating outfit were present. He was also grateful when, on reaching the bar, Dusty told the big woman who had acted as female deputy at the jailhouse that they wanted to use a side room and not be disturbed. Shown to one by the "barmaid," as the English-woman called her employees who served behind the counter, the New Englander declined the offer of a beer and started to talk when she closed the door.

"I doubt whether there's any objection to my telling you that, at the last meeting of the Commission, the British delegates asked if they could come to the railhead and see how construction is going before giving a final decision. It'll probably be all round town before nightfall."

"They do say anything that shouldn't get out *always* does, Ray," Dusty reminded. "Aren't things going well?"

"I have to admit they could be a whole lot *better*," the New Englander replied, looking uneasy. "We're still a good five miles from the Platte River in Nebraska and should be *well* beyond it by now."[1]

"How come?" Dusty asked, remembering his wife's remarks about the faith in Sangster's abilities which Harland Todhunter had expressed on more than one occasion when the construction was being discussed by the Railroad Commission. "It can't be you've been having fuss with those *Metis* from Canada we locked horns with, or anybody else, or you'd have said so before now."

"No, nobody's been making trouble for us in the way you mean," Sangster answered. "It's just—Oh hell! I may as well admit it. This's the first major construction work I've handled. In fact, it's my *first* job of any kind—!"

"Then why—?" the small Texan began, but let the question

1. *Until receiving the information upon which this book is based, we did not know the north-bound spur-line was already under construction before the Railroad Commission assembled in Mulrooney, Kansas.*

die uncompleted so as not to add to the obvious distress being
shown by the New Englander.

"Oh, I know all the theory *very* well," Sangster said bit-
terly. "And the reports on my work when I graduated from the
college were sufficiently impressive so that, because of Harland Junior's trouble, Mr. Todhunter gave me the work instead
of him."

"*Harland Junior*, huh?" Dusty said. "That'd be his son?"

"Yes!"

"Freddie said she'd heard King saying he was surprised
Mr. Todhunter was using you instead of his own son. I reckon
he'd have a pretty good reason."

"*He* considers he has. Just before we were due to graduate,
Harl was mixed up in a wild party celebrating our team winning a Boston game against Notre Dame and was kicked out.[2]
The old man was furious and disowned him, then took me up
in his place."

"So what went wrong?" Dusty inquired, although he could
guess.

"I found there is a *vast* difference in knowing the *theory*
and actually doing the job," Sangster admitted, looking down-
cast. "It takes a *special* kind of man to handle the work crews
and I've found out that I'm *not* the kind. Nor have I anybody
who *is*. Take today for example. There are two construction
crews who came into town after they were paid two days ago
and although a train's ready to take them out to the railhead, I
can't persuade them to leave the saloon where they're celebrating."

"Going by all I saw of them while I've been wearing a
badge here, those gandy dancers can do plenty of *that*," the
small Texan remarked. "Only I'd've thought that, by now,
they'd have run through their pay and be ready to head back."

"It doesn't seem like they have," the New Englander stated
in tones of annoyance. "At least, they appeared to have

2. *Based upon the variation of soccer first played at Rugby public school
in England during 1823, the "Boston game" would evolve in the United
States into "American," or "gridiron" football.*

enough to keep buying drinks at the Driven Spike Saloon when I went th—!"

"Hello, Ray," greeted Freddie Fog, having brought Sangster's explanation to an end by coming into the room. Making a prohibitive gesture as the men began to rise, she went on, "Don't get up. The barmaid told me you were here and I thought I'd look in to see if there's anything you want."

"Nothing for me, thank you," Sangster refused, after receiving an interrogatory glance from Dusty. "But I'm keeping you apart."

In her mid-twenties, Freddie was an exceptionally fine example of feminine pulchritude. Beneath a wide brimmed, low crowned black hat which was tilted rakishly to the right, her immaculately coiffured hair was coal black. Regally beautiful, her face had the rich golden tan of one in robust health. Its expression and her demeanour implied she was a person with whom, despite living in what was still very much a "man's world," it would be ill-advised to trifle or take any other kind of liberty. Instead of being dressed for appearing in her capacity as the mayor of Mulrooney, which was invariably the conventional attire of a 'good' woman by the standards prevailing in the West, she had on clothes suitable for the owner of what was claimed to be the largest and best saloon in Mulrooney. While not so revealing as the garments she wore in the evening, these emphasised the magnificently curved contours of her close to "hourglass" figure and made her a *most* attractive sight to masculine eyes.

"Don't let *that* bother you, *I'm* working even if this shiftless husband of mine has retired," the Englishwoman replied, then became more serious. "Whatever it was brought you here, it's obviously something *important* and, although I think gambling is too foolish to get in to, I'd be willing to bet it's to do with problems on the spur-line."

"It is, honey," Dusty confirmed. "Do you want to sit in on it, happen that's all right with Ray?"

"Being a nosey woman, I really only came in hoping I'd be asked," Freddie replied frankly crossing from the door and sitting down without waiting for an answer from Sangster. She removed her wide brimmed black hat and peeled the long green feather boa from around her throat, dropping them on the table, then went on, "Lord, how I *hate* wearing these!"

"It goes with the chore, honey," Dusty pointed out, bowing in mock gallantry without rising. "And you sure look *great* in them."

"Hearing *that* should tell you we're still newly-weds, Ray," Freddie asserted and, having sensed something was troubling Sangster, continued with the levity to help put him at ease. "It's either that, or my dear husband *wants* something. He only starts the sweet talk when he does, or has done something he knows I won't approve of."

"Lordy, lord, I've married me a *suspicious* kind of wife," Dusty complained in mock alarm. "Tell the boss lady what you've just told me, *amigo*. Likely she can come up with something that'll help you out."

"But it's priv—!" Sangster commenced, then made an amendment. "It's hardly right for me to inflict my troubles on *you*."

"Why not," Freddie asked with a smile, the words having been directed at her. "*Everybody* else does. You should hear some of the troubles Waco has told me about."

"Mine are probably more serious—!" the New Englander began with asperity, then looked contrite.

"I wouldn't doubt *that*," Freddie declared, showing no sign of resenting the interruption. "His most serious is having more hairs on his chest than my maid, Babsy, has on hers."

"His most serious'll be riding the blister end of a shovel when we get back to home, should he keep on about *that*," Dusty announced in a similarly light-hearted tone. Then he became more serious and continued, "Go to it, *amigo*, and we'll see what Freddie comes up with."

"And that is how things stand, Freddie," Sangster said, having repeated the gist of what he had told the small Texan. "I have to get those two crews back to work, or there isn't even the *slightest* hope of covering the distance Mr. Todhunter has led the English delegation to expect. Not that there's *much*

3. *The significance of the blond youngster's interest is explained in:* Chapter Eight, "Waco's Education," THE TROUBLE BUSTERS.

chance of it as things stand, anyway. But we might at least be able to let them see we're making progress and shouldn't be too long overdue at the junction with the Canadian line."

"They're Irish, I suppose?" Freddie guessed.

"Not all of them," the New Englander replied. "But I suppose most are. The majority of our crews are Irish."

"From what I've seen of Irish gandy dancers," Freddie assessed. "It will take more than just *asking* to get them on the work train."

"I could offer them a bonus to go back?" the New Englander suggested, as if speaking aloud to himself.

"You'd be establishing a precedent that could run into a lot of money," the Englishwoman estimated and her husband signified agreement. "Once word got out that you'd done it, they and all your other men wouldn't leave town when they came in until you'd paid another bonus."

"Then I'd better go and threaten to fire any of them who aren't on it within an hour," Sangster said, starting to push back his chair.

"*That* won't work either!" Freddie stated and Dusty nodded concurrence again. "In fact, it will only make things worse. Being Irish, particularly Irish who're drinking, it's their nature to just dig in their heels and defy you to do it."

"There's nothing more *sure* than that, *amigo*," the small Texan supported.

"If I can't order, or threaten them into going back," the New Englander groaned, looking desperate. "What's left for me to do?"

"Don't take this the wrong way, Ray," Freddie requested gently, wanting to avoid hurting the young man's feelings any more than, it was apparent, they had been already by his inability to cope with the situation causing him such concern. "But I was thinking perhaps Dusty could help you get them on the train."

"*Dusty?*" Sangster repeated, looking surprised. "You mean order them as mar—No, that won't be any good. He isn't marshal any more."

"I wasn't thinking of Dusty walking in there as marshal and ordering them to go," Freddie corrected. "That would cause bad feelings against the town and you for having asked him to take your part against them." Pausing, she looked at her husband and resumed, "Do you think the General will consider building this spur-line's pretty *important* and beneficial to the United States when he hears about it, dear?"

"Knowing him, he's already heard and does," Dusty assessed. "Fact being, happen he knew the situation, he'd tell me to do everything I could to help."

The small Texan was delighted to find, as he had anticipated, his wife was thinking along the same lines as himself without any need for them to discuss the matter. While he would have been willing to offer whatever assistance might be required to whoever was in difficulties, there was a far stronger inducement in the present circumstances. Under the strict code of honour in which he was raised from childhood, the way his life had been saved in the attempted ambush meant he was under an obligation to the man responsible. Therefore, it behooved him to respond to whatever situation arose to repay the debt.

However, regardless of his desire, Dusty was aware he no longer was a free agent. Not only did he have his duties for the OD Connected to consider, even though he was sure his uncle would have no objections to his continued absence for such a worthwhile cause, but he had also recently taken a wife from whom circumstances would compel him to separate in a short while. Knowing she had been looking forward to them spending some uninterrupted time together, as he was, he wanted her to agree with any action that could cause an even earlier departure. She had justified his faith that she would agree to him helping the New Englander. What was more, again confirming his surmise, she was steering the conversation along the lines he wanted and in a way which would prevent it appearing he was taking an unasked interest in Sangster's affairs.

"Help in what way?" the New Englander asked.

"Well," Freddie said, before the small Texan could speak. "Suppose you hired Dusty as gang boss—if that's the job I mean?" Seeing a gleam of understanding start to come in

Sangster's face, she continued, "That way, it would be *his* duty and not your's to get those crews back to work."

"But I can't ask *him* to take a job like that!" Sangster objected, despite showing hope mingled with disappointment.

"Why not?" the Englishwoman queried, bringing back her warm smile and eyeing her husband in a mock disdain. "It will get him from under my feet for a while."

"I thought you said you were going back to Texas, Dusty?" Sangster asked, looking puzzled.

"You don't reckon I'd stay on here and get talked about like *that*, now do you?" the small Texan replied, returning Freddie's look with one of the same kind. "And one of the good things about being the boss's favourite nephew is I can stay away from the spread for a spell when I'm so minded."

"But you've already been away for some time," the New Englander pointed out.

"There are *some* who would say the ranch's been running *better* for that," the beautiful young woman claimed. Again she put aside the levity and elaborated, "It makes good sense to me, Ray. You can deal with the way the construction is carried out and Dusty will see what you want gets done. It's as easy as that."

"Do either of you realize how long it will take us to reach the junction in Canada?" Sangster asked, but he was looking relieved.

"Quite a while, I would say," Freddie answered. "But Dusty won't need to go that far. Once he's got things going, you should be able to find somebody capable of replacing him and he can head back to Texas."

"That's the way I see it," the small Texan declared and held forward his right hand. "How about it, *amigo*. Do we have us a deal?"

"I'd be a damned *fool* to refuse," the New Englander stated and took the offered hand, feeling the strength of its grip even though this was not put on with the intention of impressing him. "And I'll be forever in your debt for what you're doing."

"Forget *that*," Dusty requested. "I'm deeper in your's and this'll give me a chance to pay you back."

CHAPTER SEVEN

It's *Dancing* I'm Feeling Like,
Not *Leaving*!

With the decision on how best to help Raymond Sangster made and accepted, leaving Freddie Fog to run her business, Dusty accompanied him to Phineas O'Toole's Driven Spike Saloon. When the New Englander had asked him whether they would be taking the rest of the floating outfit with them, the small Texan, knowing his acceptance as gang boss would depend upon letting it be seen he was not dependant upon anybody else for backing, had replied he did not consider there was any need to make them leave whatever diversions were occupying their attention.

Although most similar places had been quiet, the sounds of a band playing a lively jig, laughter and shouted scraps of conversation which reached the ears of the two young men as they were approaching indicated the Driven Spike Saloon was doing good business despite the sun not yet having gone down. Because of his service as town marshal, Dusty knew more about it than his companion. Situated in the vicinity of the Mulrooney depot, on the opposite side to the cattle holding pens, everything from its name to its appointments inside and out indicated the owner sought the trade of railroad workers rather than the other transient visitors from whom the population derived revenue. While run in a scrupulously honest fashion, it had acquired the reputation for being one of the toughest places in the town. In fact, so many brawls took place on the premises that there was some justification for the often repeated joke, "Did you see the new sawdust Phineas

58

O'Toole's put down in his place," which elicited the reply, "That isn't sawdust. It's last night's furniture!"

However, the small Texan knew nobody had ever been seriously injured during the fighting while he had been in office as town marshal. Nor had any of the brawls been allowed to spread from the bar-room on to the street and endanger uninvolved passers-by. What was more, knowing to have done so would have served as an open challenge sure to be taken up by the other groups—such as cowhands, buffalo hunters, or soldiers—in town, O'Toole had refused to allow the gandy dancers to hang the brass lamp from an engine outside his front entrance to signify the place was the sole province of railroad workers.

Pausing on the sidewalk, Dusty looked through a window to ascertain what he might expect when he went inside. The first thing he noticed was the owner was nowhere to be seen. Continuing the scrutiny informed him that the suggestions of celebrating to be heard while coming up were not exaggerated. Some thirty men of European origins and wearing a variety of types of clothing, except those which were favoured by and suited to the specialized needs of cowhands, were mingling with O'Toole's girls at the tables or on the space in the centre of the room left clear for dancing. All obviously had been drinking, but as far as Dusty could see, beer was the tipple instead of the more potent hard liquor which was available. Certainly he could only see schooners being held, even by the girls, or on the tables.

While the rest were strangers, Dusty recognized three as acquaintances from his earliest days as town marshal. Largest of them all in the room was, Shamus O' Sullivan, black haired, brawny and so obviously Irish he might have been painted emerald green. Almost matching him in height and heft, Fritz "Dutchy" Voigt had close cropped blond hair, Germanic features and the carriage of the Prussian soldier he had been before coming to the United States.[1] Not much taller than

1. *In the Old West, men of Germanic appearance from Holland, Germany, or Denmark, tended to be called "Dutchy" regardless of their ethnic origins.*

Dusty, slender, with dark hair and a swarthily handsome face, Louis "Frenchy" Rastignac was just as obviously Gallic by birth. Yet, despite his size—which appeared even more diminutive in his present company—Dusty knew the latter to share the unofficial leadership of the gandy dancers with the other two. He was equally aware that their reaction to his appointment as gang boss could prove crucial.

"You see what I mean?" Sangster inquired.

"I sort of expected something like this," the small Texan replied, unbuckling his gunbelt and holding it towards his companion. "Here, tote this along for me."

"But you'll be *unarmed*!" the New Englander gasped, staring from one to the other of the bone handled Colt 1860 Army Model revolvers in the holsters.

"Those *hombres* aren't gun fighters," Dusty explained, without explaining he was carrying a primitive weapon which was remarkably potent at close quarters in the right back pocket of his Levi's pants. "So going in on 'em packing iron isn't the answer."

"Then what *is*?" Sangster asked, accepting the rig with obvious reluctance.

"I'd say *that* was up to *them*," the small Texan replied as the band stopped playing and the dancers began to leave the floor. "Come on, *amigo*. Let's go get her done."

Pushing through the batwing doors with the New Englander coming after him carrying the gunbelt, Dusty strolled slowly towards the bar. The band had not commenced its next tune and all the talking died away around the room as every eye turned in their direction. While the trio of gandy dancers he had recognized and the employees of the saloon identified him, he felt sure he was a stranger to the rest except through reports of his activities as town marshal. Because he was not wearing anything to indicate his recently concluded status as a peace officer, believing him to be no more than an ordinary cowhand, they might be puzzled about why he had come into what, by this stage of a celebration, they regarded as being the private domain of workers on the railroad. Therefore, recollecting the previous visit made by Sangster, they were more interested in him. On the other hand, Dusty felt sure the locals and the trio were puzzled by seeing him enter without wearing either his badge of office or his guns.

For his part, Sangster was comparing the response of their arrival with his previous visit. Nobody had stopped talking, or even given him more than a cursory glance, on that occasion. He had had to wait until there was a lull in the music and, mounting the small raised bandstand, obtain a partial silence before he was able to announce the work train was waiting to take the gandy dancers back to their rail-head camp. Now, all of the bar-room's occupants had stopped whatever they were doing and were looking in the direction of the small Texan and himself with obvious interest. However, he did not believe for one moment that he personally was the subject of the attention. Nor did he need to wonder why this should be.

As the New Englander had observed—and envied—on other occasions, such was the strength of Dusty's personality, the crowd did not see him as small or in any way insignificant. Rather his bearing and demeanour was giving the impression that he was by far the largest person present. Most of the gandy dancers were newly arrived from the East or from working further west and had spent only a short time in Mulrooney before going to the rail-head. Therefore, they probably did not know him by sight. Nevertheless, they had an inborn respect for what they saw as being size and bulk in excess of their own. Sensing something of his true potential as a man to be reckoned with, regardless of actual feet and inches, they were waiting to discover what had brought him into their midst.

However, despite the way things were going so far, one thing puzzled and worried Sangster. He had expected the *big* Texan to enter wearing the two Colts, which he had witnessed being drawn and used with devastating speed and accuracy, as a means of enforcing the demand for an immediate return to the rail-head.

Having forgotten what he had been told at the Fair Lady Saloon about the objections to Dusty arriving armed and in an official capacity, the New Englander was unable to think of any logical reason for the discarding of the gunbelt before entering. On the other hand, he had to admit the omission did not appear to be making any great difference to the response elicited by his companion. Being employed for work requiring brawn rather than brains, few of the gandy dancers were men of intellect or given to deep thought. Nevertheless, none were so drunk they would not guess his own return heralded another demand for them to give up their pleasures and make for the work train. They would also guess, from the way he was bringing up the rear, he expected the *big* cowhand believed it was—as always happened in such situations, the majority were waiting to see the reaction from the men they regarded as their leaders. In support of the supposition, he noticed many glances were being directed at the trio of gandy dancers he knew came into that category. It was, in fact, one of them who broke the silence.

"Howdy there, *Cap'n Fog*," O'Sullivan greeted, his manner amiable and even respectful in timbre. "I hear tell's how you've been a mite *busy* of late—and not just keeping the peace among them rapscallion cowhands, blue-bellies 'n' buffler-hunters's try to disturb it."

There was an exchange of muttered comment from the crowd on hearing the name spoken with a noticeable emphasis by the burly Irishman. While the newer gandy dancers had not come into contact with the marshal of Mulrooney, they had heard enough of him to be all too aware of the reputation he had acquired and they were puzzled by his arrival with the man in charge of building the railroad. They were celebrating, but not in such a rowdy or boisterous fashion as to constitute a disturbance, so wondered if he had come to claim this was the case and order them to leave town. According to rumour and occasionally personal experience, peace officers had been employed in a similar fashion elsewhere by influential railroad bosses who met with opposition to their wishes.

"There's some would say I've been just a *mite* busy of late, Shamus, what with one thing and another," the small Texan confirmed, not commenting on the omission of railroad construction workers from the list of 'rapscallions,' but noticing that the leader of the five piece band had signalled for the others to refrain from playing. "Only I'm not hired to keep the peace in Mulrooney any longer. Marshal Kail Beauregard's took over and I've turned in my badge.''

"Then you will be taking your so lovely wife back to Texas, no, *mon Capitaine*?" Rastignac suggested, looking from Dusty to the New Englander and back with an air of puzzlement. He made a very Gallic gesture of disappointment and, although most of his audience felt sure he would not usually have been deterred by such a consideration, he went on with the air of one paying a tribute which he hoped would give no offence, "Ah, what a *pity* for Mulrooney to lose her."

"The town won't be losing her for a piece yet, Frenchie," the small Texan denied. "Way things are, she'll be keeping on running the Fair Lady for a spell."

"Not meaning any disrespect, Captain Fog," Voigt injected in his Germanic accent and it was noticeable to even the most undiscerning of the other gandy dancers that he too was speaking in a more polite and respectful manner than they would have expected. "But I thought you was a cattleman, not a saloon-keeper."

"I'm neither right now, Dutchy," Dusty corrected, knowing the crisis point was approaching. "Fact being, Mr. Sangster's hired me as *gang boss* for the railroad you gents *should* be building out to the end of track."

"*Gang boss?*" O' Sullivan repeated, glancing in the New Englander's direction and, taking in the sight of the gunbelt, he swung his gaze quickly to its owner's sides. Paying no attention to the rumble of talk which once again welled up, he nodded after a moment's thought and an exchange of looks with his companions. "So *that's* the way of it, huh?"

"That's the way of it," Dusty confirmed, deciding the Irishman and, he felt sure, the other two, had reached the correct conclusion about his presence. He was also aware that everything could depend upon their response to the issue. However, he showed nothing of his thoughts and continued in the same even tone, "And I want every last man of you on the work train in a quarter of an hour."

Keeping his gaze going around the room while the conversation was taking place, without moving his head more than a fraction in either direction—a trick he had developed as a

Cavalry officer in the War Between The States and put to good use while serving as a lawman since it ended—the small Texan studied the response to his announcement. Although O'Sullivan, Rastignac and Voigt did no more than nod in concurrence with what had clearly been an order from him, he felt certain the sentiment would not be mutual. Nor was he wrong.

"Well now," said one of a pair of obvious brothers in the forefront of the crowd, his accent labelling him as Irish. Striding into the centre of the open space with a demeanour which indicated he had drunk enough to become truculent, he went on, "Let it *never* be said's how Bob Molloy of Castlebar ever allowed *anybody* to tell him *where* he's got to go, or *when*. Hey there on the bandstand, it's *dancing* I'm feeling like, not *leaving*. Strike up a jig and may me sister marry a Protestant if I'm not still doing it in *half* an hour."

"There's always *one*!" Voigt commented dryly, watching and listening with an air of eager anticipation.

"That there *is*," Rastignac supplemented, showing just as little concern and interest over the way the situation was developing. "The *only* trouble with the Irish, *mon ami*, is that even those who can't fight *think* they can."

"Will you be shutting up, the pair of yez?" O'Sullivan requested, although there were few people from whom he would have accepted the second part of the Frenchman's comment without violent physical retaliation. "This's going to be *good*!"

Looking at Dusty while the quietly spoken exchange between the trio was taking place and receiving a quick nod of concurrence, the band leader led his musicians in a tune. Grinning in satisfaction at having his wishes respected, or so he supposed, Bob Molloy began to perform a lively and, considering his drunken state, well executed jig. However, he was not allowed to make good his boast to continue for at least thirty minutes. Picking up a nearby unoccupied chair, the small Texan sent it sliding across the patch of floor worn smooth by the feet of numerous dancers. The front of its seat caught the Irishman behind the knees as he was in the middle of a complicated step. Taken unawares, he lost his balance and sat down on the chair with a bump which caused its legs to buckle a little.

"Looks like you're plumb tuckered out already, *hombre*," the small Texan drawled, strolling forward with seeming nonchalance.

"Now *there's* a *pretty* thing!" Stewart Molloy bellowed, provoked by a desire to uphold the honour of his family and, even more, the effects of the beer he had been drinking. Exuding aggression, he lumbered unsteadily across the dance floor towards where Dusty stood facing away from him. Reaching out with his hands as he was drawing near, he continued, "I'll soon be teaching you's how you can't treat me darlin' brother that ways!"

Watching from where he had halted, Sangster suddenly returned to an awareness of the small Texan's actual size. While the approaching Irishman had nowhere near the bulk of O'Sullivan, or even his older brother, he had a height advantage of some six inches and was far from punily built. In addition to being taller and heavier, it seemed he was approaching his intended victim unexpected. However, even as the New Englander opened his mouth to yell a warning and considered drawing one of the revolvers from its holster, he discovered neither was required. What was more, it quickly became obvious that being unarmed was no impediment to Dusty's ability to protect himself.

Although the shouted threat gave added evidence that some form of hostility against him was planned, it was not entirely necessary to alert the small Texan to Stewart Molloy's intervention. Hearing the thumping of the heavy work boots on the smooth planks, Dusty realized somebody was coming and guessed it would not be a friend. Pivoting around swiftly and assessing the situation, he concluded there was no need for him to bring the potent primitive weapon from his back pocket. Instead, he took two strides towards his would-be assailant. Bringing up both hands, keeping the fingers extended together and thumbs bent across the palm in a manner different from that used in any form of fist fighting to which the rest of the room was accustomed, he used the edges to knock the outstretched arms apart. Then he grasped and bunched up the front of Stewart's shirt in both fists. Having done so, exerting a strength seemingly out of all keeping with his size, he began to push his captive backwards.

Startled by the way his jig had been brought to an end, Bob Molloy recovered sufficient of his wits to appreciate what was going on. Giving vent to a Gaellic profanity, he lurched erect. Seizing the back of the chair in both hands, he swung it up to be used as an extemporized club and started to go after his brother and Dusty. However, still being short of breath from his exertions and unexpected descent onto the chair, he did not speak to give warning that he was coming. Once again, Sangster was on the horns of a dilemma. While impressed by the way in which the younger brother was being handled, he thought the elder would prove too much for the small Texan to cope with at the same time. As previously, before the New Englander could think of how best to help, he discovered there was no need to do so.

Despite the absence of verbal verification, Dusty had something more than just approaching footsteps to warn him of danger. There was a gap in the crowd which allowed him to keep an eye on the mirror behind the bar. What he saw being reflected supplied the requisite information. Coming to a halt, with the high heels of his cowhand style boots spiking to offer a purchase against the planks as they would have on sunbaked ground if he was expecting to be subjected to powerful pulling when roping a recalcitrant animal on foot, he made another pivot. Still in the powerful grasp, the younger brother could not prevent himself being swung around. Nor, such was the timing of the response to his approach, could the elder stop his intentions.

Coming around at a close to horizontal arc, instead of finding its target, the chair struck Stewart across the shoulders. However, although his shirt was released as the blow came and he was sent in a headlong staggering sprawl, he might have counted himself fortunate in one respect. Being all too aware that the Driven Spike Saloon's reputation for brawls was well founded, its owner did not waste money by buying expensive furniture. While the kind he obtained was capable of standing up to ordinary use, it did not lend itself to being employed as a club. Therefore, the chair disintegrated on impact and inflicted far less damage than might otherwise have been the case.

Having had one assailant disposed of for him, Dusty gave his attention to the other. Before Stewart had alighted on the floor between two of the tables, the occupants having made no attempt to save him from falling, Bob received another indication that it did not pay to antagonize the *big* Texan. Swinging around, giving the older brother no time to recover from the shock caused by realizing how the attempted attack had gone badly wrong, Dusty knotted his left hand into a fist. Swinging it around and up, while stepping forward a pace to help achieve the full power of his iron hard muscles, he drove it full into the pit of the Irishman's stomach.

Despite the fact that the way in which the small Texan wore his attire tended to distract from his physical development, there was the weight of a one hundred and eighty-five pound body—none of which was fat—with its fifty inch chest slimming down to a thirty inch waist set upon thighs and calves respectively twenty-six and seventeen and a half inches in circumference, behind the blow. On the knuckles burying deep into his unprepared stomach, all the breath was expelled from Bob's lungs with a pain-filled "whoosh." His eyes bulged and his mouth opened and closed spasmodically, but soundlessly. Although his torso remained erect, his legs buckled and he collapsed to his knees. From there, clasping his hands to the point of impact, he toppled face forward to the floor and lay writhing impotently.

"Are they *yours, Mr.* O'Sullivan?" Dusty inquired, waving at his victims in a derisory fashion.

"That they are, Cap'n Fog, sir, to my everlasting shame," the massive Irishman replied. "But you'll be after having to excuse 'em. They're from County Mayo, not Donegal like me, so they don't know no better."

"They can learn on the way back to the railhead," Dusty stated. "And, as the train pulls out in fifteen minutes, you'll *all* just have time to take a *final* beer on me before you go to catch it."

CHAPTER EIGHT

He'll Be Ruined For Life

"Asking your pardon, Cap'n, sir, and don't be thinking we're ungrateful for the offer," Shamus O'Sullivan said instead of going to the bar, after having told some of the gandy dancers to take care of the Molloy brothers. "But there's still enough left over to buy us that last round and, if you'll do us the honour, to get one for your good self—and Mr. Sangster."

"Enough left over?" Dusty Fog queried, genuinely puzzled. Noticing that the inclusion of his companion had been an afterthought, it gave him an insight of how Raymond Sangster was regarded by the burly Irishman. "The railroad must be paying you right well to have money left over when you've been around town for a couple of days."

"The pay is all right, not that we couldn't use a little more," Louis 'Frenchy' Rastignac stated, darting a glance at the New Englander while making the second portion of the declaration. Being answered by a blank stare instead of a similarly light-hearted response, he swung his gaze back to the small Texan. "But you are right, *mon Capitaine*. It was little enough money we had left this morning."

"Most of us are so close to the blanket we can feel it rubbing against our hides," Fritz 'Dutchy' Voigt supplemented.

"I know the O'Toole's a generous man," Dusty drawled, swinging a look around the room and finding the occupants resuming their interrupted activities. "But, judging by the whooping it up you sounded to be doing, I wouldn't think he'd've let you have enough on the cuff until next pay day for there to be any left over by this time."

"And so he didn't," O'Sullivan confirmed. "Good man

68

though he is, he wouldn't let us go on the cuff for enough to make a bad dent in our pay next month. It'd be a round he'd give us, hearing how we was fixed, to take away the taste of the smoke from the engine on the way back and with divil the thought of being paid back. Only he wasn't here to be doing it."

"Then who did," Raymond Sangster asked.

"Some kind hearted gentlemen, *m'sieur,*" Rastignac replied, but there was a noticeable difference in his tone and his use of *'m'sieur'* had the same connotation as a Texan continuing to say 'mister' after having been introduced. The timbre of respect returned as, making it plain he was addressing Dusty, he continued, "When we called for a last beer, hopefully on the house, *mon Capitaine,* Ginty behind the bar told us a man had come in and left a hundred dollars, saying he had won a big bet on how far the spur-line had gone and wanted to stand treat for all the gandy dancers who helped him do it."

"What'd this man look like?" the small Texan asked.

"That I do not know," Rastignac admitted. "He had left before we got here. However, Ginty should be able to tell you."

"I'll ask him," Dusty decided. "And *I'll* buy the *last* round. You can let the O'Toole hold whatever's left of the bet money until the next time you come to town."

"Whatever you say, Cap'n," O'Sullivan accepted, and his two companions signified their assent to the arrangement. Then he raised his voice to a stentorian bellow. "All right now, all of yez. We've had our fun 'n' frolicking and now it's time we was headed back to work. Cap'n Fog's doing us the kindness of buying a last round, so we'll be drinking his health with it and heading for the train like he's told us."

"I hope this round counts as an expense and I get the money back," Dusty remarked to Sangster as the trio started encouraging the other gandy dancers to get and drink the beer he would be buying. "Us married men have to watch what we spend out of our own pockets, especially when it's not spent in our wife's saloon."

"I'll see you get it refunded," the New Englander promised, but with none of the levity which had accompanied the request. "*Damn* whoever it was won the bet and left the money for them to start swilling down beer."

"You should be grateful to Shamus, Frenchy and Dutchy for making sure it was only *beer* they were 'swilling down,'" the small Texan warned, realizing why Sangster had failed to establish any rapport with the gandy dancers if his attitude when in their company was always the same as it had been for the last few seconds.

"They were drinking like the rest," the New Englander protested.

"They were," Dusty conceded. "But it was only beer and they kept the others to the same instead of whiskey, or some other kind of hard liquor." Seeing Sangster looked sceptical, he elaborated, "I know those three. They're as free with their celebrating as *anybody* has a right to be after working as hard as they do. But they never let the whooping it up they've done interfere with their chores."

"Huh!" the New Englander snorted. "They didn't seem all that keen to get back to their work when I came to fetch them for the train!"

"I didn't say they were some kind of angels. Even though you're the boss of construction, you can't just walk in, start giving orders to gandy dancers and expect to have them jump to obedience, especially when there's money behind the bar to keep them in drinks. As it is, happen those three hadn't been on hand, you'd've had even more trouble in getting the rest to the work train."

"But *you*—!"

"I took out a couple of jaspers too drunk to fight properly is all."

"And after you did, nobody else has argued with what you told them!"

"Nope," Dusty conceded, beginning to realize just how little the New Englander knew about the way the men he hired thought and how to deal with them. "But, happen Shamus, Frenchy and Dutchy hadn't been willing to back me up—!"

"None of them offered to help when you were attacked," Sangster interrupted.

"They reckoned I could handle those two yahoos without

needing any help," the small Texan replied. "And knew I'd get the rest's attention real good by doing it. But I couldn't've made what I said stick anywheres near this *easy* if they'd spoke out against it. As things stand, they'll have all the rest on the work train and ready to go in just over a quarter of an hour."

"You have a lot of faith in them."

"And with good cause," Dusty declared.

"You must know them pretty well," Sangster commented.

Under the circumstances, the small Texan decided against telling the New Englander what had happened on his first contact with the trio. After they had tested him and he had won their respect by proving he was well able to defend himself without relying on guns, they had shown a willingness to remain on good terms.[1] However, although he had not seen much of them since that night, he was basing his conclusions upon his judgement of their respective characters and his summations with regards to their motives in behaving as they had since his arrival at the saloon.

"Well enough well to figure I can count on them," Dusty answered and, sensing Sangster still was not convinced, explained the reason for his belief that they were willing to give him their support. "They figured I'd be interested to hear how they all came to be drinking so copious at the *end* of a trip to town, when they should have been short of cash. Which's the why-all of Shamus offering to have the round paid for in the same way as the others had been instead of me doing the buying. He wanted us to know about the money that was left for them."

"Why?"

"Because he's got a suspicious mind, like me."

"You think the man might have had some reason when he left the money other than feeling generous after winning a bet?"

"I've heard of fellers being generous to whoever they figured had helped when they'd won a big bet," Dusty drawled. "But I don't rule out's somebody might be wanting to delay

1. *Described in:* THE MAKING OF A LAWMAN.

work on the spur-line by keeping so many men here in town."

"And you think that *Irishman* shared your suspicions?" Sangster inquired in tones of disbelief.

"He's not *stupid* and likely knows what's been doing around town since the Railroad Commission pulled in," the small Texan asserted. "And, should they have thought on those lines, him and the other two would do *everything* they could to hold the whooping up at a level where the rest would be ready to head back once the money ran out. Which, had it been whiskey and not beer they was drinking, none of them would have been in any shape to do it until tomorrow noon at the earliest."

"I'll take your word for it," Sangster said, but did not look entirely convinced. "And I won't be sorry to see them aboard and the work train going up the track."

"Or me," Dusty admitted. "So I'd best go pay for the drinks."

"I've never seen him afore, Cap'n Fog," the head bartender declared, after the small Texan had given him sufficient money to cover the cost of the round, and had then asked for information about the man who had been so beneficent. "But I mind thinking he didn't look the kind to be tossing a hundred bucks around."

"How come," Dusty inquired. "Was he a cowhand, a soldier, or a buffalo hunter?"

"Wasn't none of 'em," Ginty denied and frowned pensively. "Fact being, 'cepting he looked like a townie and not a rich 'n' at that, I'd be hard put to say *what* he was. Hell, he wasn't the kind you'd look at twice. Not so big and hefty, nor so short growed, you'd notice him on account of either. 'Bout middle-sized and middle-built you could say."

"How about his face and hair?" the small Texan asked.

"His hair was brownish and kinda long, what I could see hanging from under his derby," the head bartender answered. "But all I can remember about his face was that he'd got him a beard's covered most of it."

"I'll tell you something else, though," put in a saloon-girl who was standing close enough to have heard what was being said. "When I saw him haul out that big thick wallet, I just natural' went over to be friendly. He didn't want no company, but we was talking long enough for me to reckon he was wearing a wig and the whiskers wasn't his neither."

"Would the gal've been able to tell he was wearing a wig and false beard?" Waco asked, having listened to an account of Dusty Fog's activities on his return from the Driven Spike Saloon.

Arriving at the Fair Lady Saloon, after having seen the gandy dancers take their departure on the work train at the appointed time, Dusty had made another stop on the way, and had then found the other three members of the OD Connected's floating outfit in the bar-room with his wife. All of the cowhands had expressed an interest in what had developed and wanted to know when they would be leaving for the rail-head. On being asked how they had heard of what he was planning to do, Waco had stated a "little bird" had told them and, darting a pointed look at her vivacious little blonde maid —whose current attire was that of a saloon-girl rather than a domestic servant—Freddie had said dryly, "It must have been a Cockney sparrow." Business had improved since the small Texan left with Raymond Sangster, so Freddie had suggested they continued their discussion in the privacy of her living quarters on the first floor; to which access could only be gained from the rest of the building by a single door. Taking them to the luxuriously furnished sitting-room and telling them to sit down, she had supplied refreshments and listened to what her husband had to say.

"She reckoned's how she'd been in the theatre long enough to tell," the small Texan replied. "And Ginty backed her up."

"You *can't* be figuring this *hombre* down to the Driven Spike and the one's took on those three yahoos to try and gun Dusty down's one and the same," the Ysabel Kid put in, as if he did not have thoughts along the same lines. "Now can you, boy?"

"Nope," Waco replied, but his tone was dripping with bla-tant sarcasm. "The whole god-dam—*dad-blasted*—State of Kansas's just a-crawling with *hombres* who run 'round wear-ing wigs 'n' false whiskers. Man can't even walk a couple of yards without being hip deep in 'em. Why they're thicker'n fleas—!"

"I reckon you've made your point, boy," Mark Counter drawled from the comfortable armchair where he was lounging. "Don't ride it from here to there and back the long way."

"Well now!" Freddie put in, eyeing the youngster in mock gravity and amused at the amendment to his heated declaration made out of deference to her presence. "I didn't think anybody else had noticed how you do tend to go *on* just a trifle when you're excited, dear boy."

"Now me," the Kid supplemented. "I'd've thought *everybody* in these whole god-dam—*dad-blasted*—United States of America'd noticed *that*."

"Like I was saying." Waco drawled with an aura of patient martyrdom, but alert to hurriedly leave the chair he had selected if any kind of physical objections should be taken against him. "It strikes a poor lil ole country boy like me's *mighty* surprising *two* jaspers'd both be running around with wigs 'n' false beards."

"Could be one of 'em didn't want to be fixed so somebody could come up and say, 'Howdy, you-all. Didn't you take me on to go after Cap'n Dustine Edward Marsden "Dusty" Fog with a gun?' should the bushwhacking've come off," the Kid suggested. "And tuther wouldn't be no more eager to have, 'Howdy, you-all. Aren't you the jasper's handed over a hundred simoleons to keep some gandy dancers from going back to work on the railroad,' throwed at him."

"I always thought Indians were men of few words," Freddie commented with a sigh.

"Lon *sometimes* is," Dusty informed his wife, knowing the Kid was proud of his Indian blood and never objected to it being mentioned in a seemingly derisive fashion by good friends.

"But not often enough and they *never* make any sense, long or short," Waco asserted, despite realizing the black dressed Texan had made a good point. "They could be the same feller trying to make things go bad for the spur-line. With Dusty out of the way, those gandy dancers'd likely still be whooping it up at the Driven Spike no matter what Shamus

O'Sullivan, Frenchy and Dutchy said or did to get 'em on the train."

"There's just one lil thing wrong with that," the small Texan warned, pleased—as were Mark and the Kid—by the way in which the youngster was once again showing a capability for thinking matters out. It was a vastly different, greatly improved, outlook to that of their first meeting.[2] "I'd hardly said two words at a go to Ray Sangster, much less offered to help him out, when those three yahoos came after me. Top of which, having been riding the same trail as you on this disguise business, I called in at the jailhouse and talked to Meacher. He insisted that, while there wasn't any reason actually given for wanting me made wolf bait, the *hombre* who took them on was taller and better built than him."

"Now to a poor lil ole part-Comanch' boy like me," the Kid drawled, eyeing Waco sardonically. "It seems they're either two different *hombres,* else it's just one jasper's found some slick way of growing bigger or littler as he's so minded."

"By the way, dear," Freddie put in, before the youngster could think up a suitably sarcastic reply. "Does Meacher know you aren't going to press charges against him and he'll be released tomorrow?"

"Released?" Waco yelped, almost rising, and the other two cowhands came nearly as close to showing their surprise.

"We've decided it's for the *best,*" Freddie explained. "I've seen him and, while I wouldn't say he was over intelligent, I feel he's smart enough to have learned his lesson from what's happened. If he stands trial for attempted murder, the judge will send him to the State Penitentiary for quite a few years—!"

"And so he *should* be, the lousy son-of-a-bi—!" the youngster interrupted, but was not so filled with righteous indignation over what he considered great leniency being shown to the attempted killer of the man he admired more than anybody else in the world that he entirely forgot the presence of the beautiful Englishwoman.

2. *Told in:* TRIGGER FAST.

"I don't agree," Freddie stated gently, guessing and approving of the reason for the outburst. "Oh, I know he shouldn't have got involved with the ambush, but I'm convinced he let the other two lead him into it rather than doing the leading himself. Now he's had a very bad fright from seeing his two friends killed and being wounded himself. What happened at the jail has shown him that, no matter how he might have felt before, he isn't smart enough to be a successful outlaw and it could make him willing to consider honest work is best. But if he stands trial and goes to the Penitentiary, he'll be ruined for life. With the treatment he'll get and the company he'll be keeping, he'll come out either so broken in spirit that he'll be useless for *anything*, or he'll have become hardened enough to start on the owlhoot trail."

"I reckoned he'll be way too smart to try coming after Dusty again once he's loose," Waco commented, being willing to accept the decision as the beautiful Englishwoman and the small Texan were obviously in favour of it. Then a hopeful tone came into his voice and he continued, "How's about it happen I'm waiting 'round the back of the jailhouse when he's turned loose and sort of whomp him on his lil ole pumpkin head a few times to make sure he *has* learned his lesson?"

"And you talk about us Injuns being mean!" the Kid sniffed, amused as were the others by the display of loyalty.

"Hasn't he got a *brain*?" Mark seconded, having similar emotions. "Or should that be *has* he got a brain?"

"Don't let those two *bully* you, dear boy," Freddie said and crossed to pat Waco's blond head. "I think you're simply *wonderful*."

"Time had to come when somebody did," Dusty declared. "I only wish it hadn't been my *wife*. Anyways, you fellers'd best go back to whatever you was doing and get on doing it. I'll be going out to the railhead comes morning and, knowing you, I figure you'll be wanting to come with me."

CHAPTER NINE

I Thought You'd *Never* Ask

"Whee-Dogie!" the Ysabel Kid ejaculated, bringing his horse to a halt. To anybody who knew him as well as did three of his audience, it was obvious that the news that had just been imparted to him was causing considerable perturbation. "You mean we-all've got to go on *this*?"

"It'll get us to the railhead a whole heap quicker than riding," Dusty Fog replied, although he could see the difficulties which might arise if they adopted the means of transportation under consideration. Glancing at the small crowd of railroad employees, and the usual loafers with nothing better to do, who had gathered and were watching, he went on, "Ray says they've got a railroad car fixed up specially for carrying horses."

Taking a dinner with Raymond Sangster in a side room at the Fair Lady Saloon the previous evening, while the other three members of the OD Connected's floating outfit were celebrating with their respective favourites amongst his wife's girls in the bar-room, the small Texan had learned something of how the construction work was carried out and about the various problems which had led to the delays. He had been too polite to say so, but he considered most of the latter were caused by poor organization and leadership rather than bad luck. However, he knew that he could not decide whether this was the case until he had seen the work being carried out. Stating he and his *amigos* would be ready to go to the railhead the following day, he was informed they could travel by the supply train in which the New Englander would be returning. Dusty had pointed out one major difficulty with this means of travel, but had been told there were special facilities available which offered an answer to the problem. Joining his wife, Mark Counter, the Ysabel Kid and Waco at the conclusion of the meal, Sangster having declined his offer to do so, Dusty had put the matter from his mind after he had told them of the arrangements he had made. He had noticed the youngster in particular looked pleased by the possibility of having such a novel experience.

That morning, at Freddie Fog's suggestion, the Texans had packed such of their belongings as they thought would be needed while at the railhead, and had left the remainder in her quarters until they returned. Going to the livery barn where they had accommodated their horses and stored their saddles, they had made ready for setting out. Assuming they would be going on horseback as usual and without noticing that Dusty did not have his with him, the other three had strapped the war bags containing those of their "thirty years" gatherings' they felt might be required and bedrolls—wrapped in waterproof tarpaulin "tarps" as protection against the elements—to the cantles of their low horned, doubled girthed saddles. Nor, after having controlled the friskiness shown by the animals as a result of a period of good food and light exercise, did the arrival of Freddie and her maid in a buggy cause them to revise their opinion. However, on reaching the sidings near the railroad depot, they had discovered they were wrong in their assumption with regard to the way they would be making the journey.

As usual, the train which was waiting was comprised of— from the rear—a caboose—the domain of the brakeman and conductor—a comfortably furnished Pullman Pioneer car converted into combined office and living quarters for Sangster, a less luxurious "day coach" for passengers not considered important enough to ride with him, three flat cars loaded with rails and other equipment, three trucks carrying coal, and a fuel tender. However, having been told that Dusty and the other Texans would be taking their mounts, the New Englander had had inserted between the goods and passenger sections what a later generation would call a "horse box" which was constructed to specifications he was given on reaching

Mulrooney. The train was drawn by a standard American Type engine built at the Grant Locomotive Works in Paterson, New Jersey. Described as a 4-4-0 in the American Whyte formula, it was four-coupled with a leading bogie truck supporting outside cylinders and equipped as a wood-burner. While not the latest and most modern of its class, it showed signs of having been well maintained by its driver and fireman and was capable of doing all that was required.

"I've seen inside it, Lon," Freddie said, descending from the driving seat of the buggy while the maid was dismounting with an equal ease. Without explaining it was she who had given instructions for the way the car was fitted for its purpose, she went on, "It's quite well equipped, considering we're over here in the 'colonies,'[1] and we often send even valuable hunters and race horses in such boxes back in England."

"Well now," Waco drawled, after dismounting and making sure he was beyond the reach of the beautiful Englishwoman. "Whatever you Lime-Juicers can do over there, us Texans can do a heap better."

"You watch what you're saying, *mate*!" Barbara "Babsy" Smith warned in her strident Cockney voice, looking around from where she was securing the buggy's horse by attaching a rope with a heavy lead weight at the bottom end to the bridle. "Blokes've had all the hairs pulled out of their chests for saying things like *that*!"

In her own way, the speaker presented just as attractive an appearance as her employer. Barely over five foot in height, roughly the same age as Freddie, she had tightly curled blonde hair taken in a pile on top of her head. Her face was pretty, with an expression indicative of a vivacious nature and a love of life. Although she had put on less revealing clothes than

1. *Like many of her generation and class Freddie Fog, despite being married to a Texan and classed for legal purposes as an American citizen, often expressed the belief albeit a trifle tongue-in cheek that the world was divided into two parts, Great—as it was then—Britain and its colonies. Therefore, she claimed, anywhere outside the British Isles was a "colony." For our feelings on this point of view; see the dedication for:* KILL DUSTY FOG!

she wore when working in the bar-room, they were far from being as decorous as the uniform she wore in her capacity of maid. A trifle more brilliantly coloured than fashion dictated for a "good" woman, the attire fitted so snugly it did nothing to hide the rich curves of her firmly fleshed close-to-buxom figure. Having formed a regular twosome with Waco, because of her volatile spirits, their relationship had become a source of considerable amusement to Freddie and the other members of the floating outfit.

"And it would serve you *right,* too," Freddie asserted, then gestured towards the horse box. "Why don't you lead the way, darling?"

Despite the horses' owners having been raised around the animals almost from the cradle like most Texans, the beautiful Englishwoman knew that loading and persuading the animals to accept such unaccustomed conditions while travelling was far from a sinecure. They were bred for travelling long distances at a high average speed, rather than working cattle, and none was much under seventeen hands. In the peak of condition, due to having been resting and grain-fed for most of the time the men were acting as peace officers, each was powerful enough to cause serious trouble should it become disturbed or alarmed. If that was true of Dusty's and Waco's paints—the latter bearing the CA brand of Clay Allison's *remuda* and having been selected on leaving that outfit because his hero rode one—and Mark's slightly larger bloodbay, it applied all the more to the Kid's magnificent white stallion. Biggest of the quartet, caught and trained by him, it still possessed much of its *manadero* herd stallion's wild nature.

However, Freddie realized her husband and his companions had one thing in their favour. Accepting that railroads were going to spread all over the country and wanting to be prepared for that day, they had regularly taken time from their duties at the town marshal's office to bring their horses around the depot. By doing so, they had allowed the animals to grow accustomed to the sound of trains and none were now particularly perturbed when near one. On the other hand, she appreciated that getting them aboard the car and keeping them under control while it was in motion would prove a very different matter.

"I thought you'd *never* ask," the small Texan assented, Freddie's last words having been addressed to him. Dismounting, he continued, "Let's get them on ready to go, *amigos*."

"We could allus ride out a ways to kind of work some of the bed-springs out of their bellies afore we got on, Dusty," Waco suggested, rubbing the sleek neck of his big paint, but refraining from dismounting.

"That'd be a right smart notion, 'cepting for one thing, boy," Mark commented, tossing his right leg over the saddle-horn as a preliminary to dropping to the ground. Thinking the sturdy wire rope on either side was there to help hold it steady, he waved a hand to the wooden ramp which slanted from the ground to the entrance of the car and went on, "We wouldn't have this dingus to help us was we to do it."

"You would," Freddie corrected. "It hauls up and forms the door while you're moving."

"They'll likely be easier to handle here than out on the range, anyways," Dusty estimated, having already considered and discarded the proposal made by the youngster while thinking of the transportation problem on his way to the depot. He noticed the somewhat anticipatory way in which the spectators were watching and listening, and realized that he in particular was being subjected to a test. It would hardly enhance his authority if word spread that, although going to be gang boss in charge of the building crews at the railhead, he could not even take his horse into the car. "Let's get our rigs off and take a look inside."

Having removed and carried their saddles up the ramp, leaving the horses standing "ground hitched" by allowing the split-ended reins to dangle from the bridles, the Texans looked around and approved of what they saw. The car had excellent ventilation, and on either side of the entrance were three stalls which were fixed parallel to the line of the rails. Each was just wide enough for the horse to stand in comfort and yet be restrained from moving around. Offering a more secure footing than would either the bare boards or a layer of straw, sand covered the floor to a depth of two or three inches. The dividing walls and the wooden bar serving as a gate were lined with straw-padded burlap. Although there was a sturdy manger, no trough for water was provided. However, there was an adequate supply in a barrel and several buckets in which it could be taken to the horses. A wooden rack upon which the saddles could be hung instead of laid on the floor or hung by a stirrup iron was supplied and a couple of benches for the men who would be accompanying the animals.

"Give Mr. Sangster his due, 'though I wouldn't've expected him to have so much savvy," Mark drawled, hanging up his rig with the bed roll still attached and the Winchester Model of 1866 rifle pointing forward in its boot on the left side. "He's fitted this out pretty good."

"I'll float my stick with you on that, *amigo*," Dusty admitted, noticing how the blond giant had employed the word 'mister' instead of using the New Englander's given name, thus making a statement which would not have been uttered if there was a liking between them. Instead of commenting on the matter, having placed his saddle on the rack, he reached up to unfasten his bandana and went on, "But I reckon we'd best cover the horses eyes before we make a stab at it getting them in."

Although Mark and Waco duplicated the actions of their leader on leaving the box, the Kid had no need to do so. By drawing down the three inches wide browband of the hackamore he preferred instead of a conventional bridle, he dispensed with the need to use his black bandana as a blindfold for the white stallion. Of course, he could not allow the opportunity to pass of commenting upon the advantage he gained.

"I allus said you fellers should use the right kind of rig," the black dressed Texan announced. "But you *never* listen."

"What did he say, Mark?" Waco inquired, looking around from where he was using his opened out bandana to cover the eyes of his paint.

"I dunno," the blond giant replied, ensuring his bloodbay —its coat the rich deep red colour of old mahogany—would be unable to see while it was being taken into the car. "I *never* listen to *anything* he says, nor *you* for that matter."

Smiling at the exchange of comments between the other three, knowing it was made partly to relieve a tension similar to that he was experiencing, Dusty accepted one of the lead ropes his wife had brought in the buggy. Then, taking the reins, he led his big paint stallion towards the ramp. Despite the blindfold, being well trained, it followed him without making any resistance while on level ground. However, feeling the planks beneath its hooves and hearing the different sound they made, it showed signs of nervousness. Speaking in a quiet and soothing tone, he kept it moving upwards and into the car. Taking it to the right hand stall at the left side of the doorway, he persuaded it to enter and removed the bit. Having tied it short by the head, using the lead rope, he withdrew and lowered the padded wooden bar into place behind it. By the time he was finished, Mark arrived and, putting the bloodbay next to Dusty's horse, secured it in the same fashion. Nor, because of their skill in matters equestrian and the rapport established with the white and other paint, did the Kid and Waco have any greater difficulty in getting them aboard and accommodating them.

On leaving the car, after removing the blindfolds and spending a few seconds helping the horses to become accustomed to their unusual surroundings, the Texan found the distaff side of their party talking with a burly white man in a peaked cap and bib-overalls and a shorter, heavily built Negro dressed in a similar fashion.

"Dusty, boys," Freddie said. "This is Tom Riordan and Moses Jones, the engineer and fireman of the train."

"Glad to know you, Cap'n Fog, gents," the white railroad man declared and his companion nodded a cheerful greeting, "Being a right law-abiding and upright sort of a feller—and knowing my wife'd whomp me over the head with a broomhandle should I have got tossed in the pokey 'n' fined—our paths never crossed while you was marshal. Anyways, Mose and me'll get you to the railhead a heap faster'n you could ride there."

"Why sure," Dusty drawled, although he observed with some amusement that the words were directed more to Mark than himself. It was an error people had often made in the past and, he did not doubt, would continue to do so. "After what I've told the boys, I'm counting on you to do that or I'll never live it down."

"Tom says he'll go easy on the whistle and try not to do too much jerking until those fool horses of yours get used to riding the car," Freddie said, after the brief moment of embarrassment had passed due to Riordan discovering the mistake in identification he had made. He and the fireman then shook hands with her husband. She did not mention the suggestion had come from her, but glanced away and continued, "Here comes Raymond Sangster."

"We'd best be going to the Colonel, Mose," the engineer announced, darting a look in the same direction, his tone suggesting to Dusty that he too was not enamoured of the New Englander.

"The Colonel?" Waco queried, before the men could leave.

"That's what we call our old engine," Riordan explained. "'Cause you Johnny Rebs took the General back from our boys in the War."[2]

"Those Southern gennelmen'd never've got him back had me 'n' you been on the foot-plate, boss," Jones asserted with a grin, but watched carefully for any resentment on the part of the Texans that might be caused by his comment.

"Likely not," Dusty drawled amiably and the others also showed no animosity. "'Course, Jim Andrews didn't have the Texan Light Cavalry after him, or the chase he led would've been some shorter."

"And shorter still had it been ole General Bushrod Sheldon's boys," Mark supplemented, having served with the outfit he named.

"He wouldn't even got *near* the railroad had Colonel Mosby been around with pappy and me riding scout," the Kid boasted.

2. *During the War Between The States, accompanied by volunteers from various Federal Army regiments, Union spy James J. Andrews attempted to steal a Southern passenger train, but failed due to the efforts of its conductor, William A. Fuller. The incident formed the basis of the plot for the Walt Disney movie,* THE GREAT LOCOMOTIVE CHASE, *released in 1956.*

"Danged if we're not surrounded by Johnny Rebs," Riordan informed Jones in mock horror. "Let's get to the Colonel afore they takes it prisoner's well."

"Glad to see you're all here," Sangster greeted, striding up and glaring after the departing engineer and fireman. "We're due to be leaving in a few minutes. Shall I have your gear put in my Pullman, Dusty?"

"Nope, thanks," the small Texan refused. "I'll be riding in the box to keep an eye on my horse."

"But surely your men could do that?" the New Englander inquired, glancing at the three cowhands.

"They've got their own to look out for," Dusty replied, just a trifle coldly, realizing the invitation had been meant for him alone.

"Very well," Sangster assented. "I'll go and board."

"You know something," Mark drawled, watching the New Englander walk away. "For all he saved you in that bushwhack, Dusty, I just can't *take* to that fell—!"

"What the *hell*!" Waco snapped, breaking in upon the blond giant's comment with a savage ejaculation and his right hand dipped towards the staghorn grip of his off side Army Colt.

Dave Short Wants You

Looking around, the two Englishwomen and the rest of the Texans had no trouble discovering the reason for Waco's words and action. Michael Meacher was approaching through the crowd of onlookers, all of whom were showing signs of disappointment that the loading of the horses had failed to produce any dramatic display. At the sight of the staghorn handled revolver, which came into the blond youngster's right hand with a speed indicating much practice and suggesting a similar ability at shooting accurately, most of the spectators, even those who had not heard of his competence in such matters, hurriedly scattered. However, the cause of the reaction skidded to a halt and, accepting the pain caused to his injured shoulder, jerked his hands into the air.

It was obvious from the would-be hired killer's appearance that, although he had not been subjected to any physical abuse, his sojourn in the jailhouse had left its mark. Beneath the stubble on his cheeks, his face was pale and haggard. Despite having been fed adequately during his confinement, he had lost weight and his clothes were hanging somewhat baggily. Although the rest of his attire was the same, he was wearing a shirt out of his warbag—recovered by the peace officers along with the property of his dead companions from the horses they had left at the rear end of the alley where they waited for their intended victim—to replace the one damaged when Doctor Brian Farnsworth gave first aid to his wounded shoulder. However, his gunbelt and its two Colt 1860 Army Model revolvers were conspicuous by their absence.

"H—hold hard th—there!" Meacher requested in a quavering voice.

"What the hell do you want?" Waco demanded, retaining the Army Colt's barrel in a rock steady alignment and holding back the hammer with his thumb while keeping the trigger depressed by his forefinger.

"T—To see Cap'n Fog," replied the survivor of the abortive ambush. "I—I'm not toting a g—gun!"

"Come ahead," the small Texan commanded, feeling sure the assertion was correct.

"What the devil is *he* doing here?" Raymond Sangster demanded, striding back quickly and pointing at the newcomer. "Has he *escaped* from the jail?"

"Hey!" Meacher yelped before the question could be answered, staring at the New Englander. "You're the one—!"

"The one who what?" Waco demanded, still without having lowered his revolver.

"Who—!" Meacher began, then paused for a few seconds before continuing, "Who—Who hoodwinked me that night in the jailhouse."

"That wasn't *difficult*," Sangster sniffed disdainfully. "But why isn't he still being held there?"

"He's been turned loose," Dusty Fog replied, the words being directed his way.

"Turned *loose*?" the New Englander repeated, sounding as if he could not believe his ears.

"That's right," the small Texan confirmed. "I've decided not to have him brought to trial."

"Why ever *not*?" Sangster asked, looking at Meacher and finding he was being subjected to a scrutiny he assumed to be caused by awe over the memory of the successful deception he had achieved when they were together in the cell.

"For one thing," the small Texan drawled, employing a reason he felt sure would be most acceptable to the New Englander. "If he was hauled in front of the judge, I'd have to stay on in town to be a witness—And that would mean I couldn't come with you to the railhead until the trial was over."

"I can see that," Sangster conceded and gave a shrug. "Well, you know *best*. But why has he come *here*?"

"I was just going to ask," Dusty admitted, then glanced at the blond youngster. "Leather it!"

"Yo!" Waco replied, giving the traditional cavalry assent to an order. Relaxing his forefinger and allowing the hammer to sink on to the safety notch between the two uppermost percussion caps on the chamber under the control of his thumb, he twirled away the long barrelled Army Colt almost as swiftly as it was drawn. A timbre of warning came into his voice as he raised his empty hand, "I can right *easy* get it out again, should it be *needed*."

"It *won't* be," Dusty asserted and gave his attention to the newcomer. "Well, what does bring you here?"

"I—I—!" Meacher began, swinging his gaze from Sangster with what appeared to be reluctance. "I wanted to thank you afore you left town for making 'em turn me loose, Cap'n Fog."

"How'd you know where to find me?" the small Texan inquired, showing none of the surprise he felt at the expression of gratitude.

"The new marshal told me," Meacher replied.

"Huh huh!" Dusty grunted. "And what've you got in mind to do now you're free?"

"Get me some work to raise enough money so's I can head back home," Meacher answered and, once more, his gaze flickered on the New Englander.

"There's none for *you* on the railroad," Sangster stated bluntly.

"I didn't want none, mister," Meacher corrected. "It'd take me further away from home. I'm looking for something around town."

"I'll see what I can do to help you get something," Freddie Fog promised and, having a strong sense of justice, she tried to decide which of her associates had the hardest and least salubrious jobs which could be handed out as punishment to the young man.

"Thank you kindly, ma'am," Meacher replied, bringing his gaze back to the beautiful Englishwoman after it had gone to Sangster again. "I can use some help, I reckon. And a place to stay, only I don't have no money to get one."

"Sell your gunbelt and guns," Freddie suggested. "They helped get you into trouble and you aren't likely to need them on your way home."

"Nope, I don't reckon I am, ma'am," Meacher admitted. "Only folks around town might not want to let me have a place to stay on account of what I let myself get talked into trying to do."

"I'll do what I can about getting you somewhere," Freddie declared, ignoring the suggestion of a less willing part in the attempted ambush than she suspected had been the case. "Go and wait for me at the Fair Lady Saloon. Tell the barmaid I said you're to have some hot water for a shave and you can have a meal on the house."

"That's real good of you, ma'am," Meacher asserted.

"It's nothing," Freddie said.

"It's time for the train to leave," Sangster announced, before anything more could be said. "We'll have to be getting aboard."

"Why sure," Dusty agreed and took his wife in his arms. "I'll see you as soon's I can, honey."

"Of course, dear," the beautiful Englishwoman replied, and she gestured to a nearby post supporting the glinting wire of the telegraph line which ran parallel to the tracks as far as the railhead. "I'll send you any news that comes in."

"*Bueno*," the small Texan said, then gave Freddie a kiss. "And I'll do the same for you should there be anything worth telling."

"You'd *better*," the Englishwoman warned with a mock severity. Nodding to where her maid was being accorded similar treatment by Waco, she went on with a smile, "Babsy and I'll come up on the work train for a weekend in a couple of weeks—If that will be all right with you, Raymond?"

"Yes," Sangster answered, wishing Meacher would stop staring at him with an expression of what appeared to be disappointment and which he could not account for. "That will be all right."

"*Bueno*," Dusty drawled, being too absorbed in taking his departure to notice Meacher's behaviour. Nor, with the moment of leave-taking at hand, did any of his *amigos*. "Look after yourself, honey."

"And you, dear," Freddie requested, stepping away. "I hope it isn't too long before you can come back."

"And me," the small Texan seconded, then he turned and followed his three companions up the ramp into the horse box.

Having withdrawn to an alley, Michael Meacher watched with mixed emotions as the train pulled out of the depot and the Englishwoman climbed into the buggy to drive away. Then, disappointed by one aspect of the departure, he turned and walked off.

That morning, on being told the reason he was to be re-leased and would not stand trial by the new town marshal of Mulrooney, Meacher had been surprised but delighted. When Kail Beauregard had questioned him about his plans for the future, realizing they were subject to revision in the light of what was happening, he had thought quickly and given much the same explanation as he had just repeated to Freddie and Dusty Fog. Instructed to watch his behaviour, he had learned the whereabouts of the small Texan by announcing his desire to apologise for being part of the ambush and to express his gratitude. Admitting this would be a good gesture, the marshal had supplied the information and stated he could return to collect his belongings after he had done so. Having no inten-tion of attempting offensive action against the *big* Texan, in what he knew would prove a vain hope to avenge his dead companions, he had not felt in the least concerned because his gunbelt and revolvers were included in the property retained at the jailhouse.

Freddie had been partially correct in her assumptions about how Meacher would react to his captivity and the possibility of a much longer, far less easy going, incarceration in the State Penitentiary after his trial. However, she had not known he had been sustained by a belief that he might be able to get a reduction in his sentence. Commencing on the day he and his companions arrived in Mulrooney, while Ronald "Rocky" Todd was contacting their employer and William Dougal

"Bad Bill" Hamilton wasted the last of their money gambling at a saloon, he had come into possession of some information he had felt sure he could trade with Dusty Fog to obtain leniency.

When Meacher had reached the railroad depot, there had been a most unexpected development which at first led him to wonder if he was going to be able to benefit from the information he had. Then, in the light of what he had seen and heard, he had with a speed which would have surprised his deceased companions, drawn a shrewd conclusion. His companions, like other people, had always tended to regard him as a dim witted hanger-on to their schemes. Deciding there could be more profit if he employed his knowledge in a different way, he had appreciated the need to remain in Mulrooney for an indefinite period before he could put his new plan into effect. While not enamoured of the prospect of having to work for his living in the interim, he was grateful to the beautiful Englishwoman for her offer of assistance in finding accommodation and employment. He suspected that without either he would soon be considered a vagrant and ordered to leave by the marshal.

"Hey," a harsh voice growled with a Mid-West accent. "You're Ronnie Todd's sidekick, Meacher, ain't you?"

Jolted from his reverie by the words, the survivor of the failed ambush found himself confronted by two men. Somewhat taller and more heavily built than himself, with low tied revolvers in better designed gunbelts than he had ever owned, they had on none too clean range clothes. However, the garments were of good quality and the grime was the result of long travelling in the open air rather than from having been worn while working cattle. Unshaven for a few days, their faces had a hardness and menace which he would have found disconcerting and frightening even if he had been armed. They were in fact, the kind of tough looking hard-cases he and his companions had always sought to give the impression of being.

"Th—That's my name," Meacher admitted worriedly.

"We heard tell's how you was siding Todd in the bushwhack when he got killed by Dusty Fog," growled the taller of the pair. "Only you came through it just nicked by a bullet 'n' was hauled off to the pokey."

"I was," Meacher confirmed.

"So how come you're roaming around loose?" the man inquired suspiciously.

"I got let out," Meacher answered, but was not allowed to continue.

"How come?" the shorter of the pair demanded.

"Cap—*Dusty* Fog's got him took on with the railroad as a hired gun, or some such, and didn't want to have to stay around town for the trial," Meacher explained, wondering if he had fallen into the hands of a couple of bounty hunters who believed he had escaped from the jailhouse and thought they might procure a reward if he was returned. "So his missus, she's mayor and—!"

"We *know* who she is," the shorter man stated coldly. "And *what!*"

"Well," Meacher said. "Being who she is and having so much pull around town, she passed the word for the new marshal to turn me loose 'n' he did."

"Did, huh?" the shorter man said in a tone of disbelief.

"Yes!" Meacher confirmed, looking around nervously and finding there was nobody else in sight. "I— I'll c—come to the jailhouse with you so's you can ask the marshal if I'm telling you the truth."

"You're coming with us, all right," the taller man declared. "But not to see no god-damned tin-star marshal."

"Wh—Wh—Where're we going?" Meacher forced himself to ask, made more alarmed by the cold hostility with which he was being watched.

"Dave Short wants you," the taller man explained.

"D—*Dave Short*?" Meacher repeated and, in his state of peturbation it took a moment for the implication of the name to sink in. "Isn't he—Rock—Ronnie Todd's uncle."

"That's just who he be," the shorter man agreed with a mixture of contempt and menace in his attitude. "Which he's wanting to know how come his favourite nephew got made wolf bait and you're still alive."

"And I just hope you've got a damned good *reason* to give him," the taller went on, his demeanour similar to that of his companion. "Because, happen you *haven't*, you're going to wish you'd got made wolf bait 'long of the other two.

CHAPTER ELEVEN

This Isn't *Fun*!

"It's not much further now," Raymond Sangster announced. He was sitting a horse taken from those kept available for such purposes at the work camp, and was accompanying Dusty Fog and, to his annoyance at their insistence upon being included in the party, the other three Texans. They were riding to where the construction of the spur-line was taking place. He did not give any expression of the relief he was experiencing, at the thought that the journey was nearly over, but it was implied by his tone. Being an indifferent rider at best, he would rather have made the journey on a hand-car; preferably with some-body to work the pump-like handles which supplied the mo-tive power. "We should see it over the next rise."

Having made the journey to the railhead without incident, albeit much faster than they could have travelled on horse-back, the Texans had found something like a small town erected where the single track had points and a siding equipped to allow the engines to turn around. Further along, another siding had four converted passenger cars, to which the one used by the New Englander would be added. Two served as storehouses for the smaller and perishable items of equip-ment, or those which might easily be stolen. Like Sangster's Pullman, the other pair were used as accommodation and of-fices for the men in charge of construction. To the south of the siding were numerous tents, or simple shanties made from wooden boards and tarpaulin roofs, supplying living quarters for the gandy dancers and others engaged in the manual labour of laying the rails. Between the two sidings, a couple of large pole corrals held a number of horses either for riding or use in harness. There were some sturdy freight wagons and lighter, basically passenger carrying, vehicles for transportation away from the truck.

One contretemps, stemming from the lack of concern Sangster showed where anything to do with those he felt below his social status was concerned, had risen on arrival. Taken and shown where he would be quartered with the surveyors and other high grade employees in one of the converted passenger cars, Dusty had noticed that although there were half a dozen empty cubicles, there was no mention by the New Englander of Dusty's three companions making use of any of them. When the matter was raised by the small Texan, the New Englander, making it obvious that the need to provide accommodation for them had not occurred to him, had given his grudging consent for them to be housed. Seeing the annoyance shown by Mark Counter, the Ysabel Kid and, in particular, Waco—although it would not have been discernible to anyone who did not know them well—Dusty had suggested they put away their belongings, then give their horses some exercise by riding out to see what was being done further up the line. Sangster had suggested he accompanied them in a manner which implied he doubted whether they could find the area without his guidance. They had ridden in a northerly direction across the undulating open range parallel to the track already laid.

"I thought I could hear *something*," Waco commented dryly, although he and, he felt sure, the other members of the floating outfit had been listening to various noises suggesting they were drawing close to their destination for some time. "Only I wasn't real *sure* about it."

"Looks like you're following an old buffalo trail," Dusty said, worried by the latest evidence that the blond youngster did not care for Sangster.

"Why sure," the Kid concurred, also having been studying the signs indicating the spur-line was being constructed along a route originally taken by the once numerous herds of buffalo. Although sure his *amigos* had reached a similar conclusion, he continued, "Only, seeing's the buffalo're long gone from hereabouts, a fair slew of some other kind of critters've been using it more recent' than that."

"I've heard tell's how they raised *cattle* up north here like we do in Texas," Waco remarked, sounding as if he gave little credence to the story. "You figure that's the truthful-true, Dusty?"

"They raise cattle, like we do," the small Texan confirmed.

"Only not's *good,* nor's *many,*" drawled the blond youngster, full of a Texan's pride in his home State.

"Likely got the notion for doing it when they saw how much money us Texans was making from it," Mark went on. "Fact being, I've got an uncle's came to show 'em how and runs him a fair sized spread up somewheres beyond the Platte."

"You Counters show up *everywhere,*" the blond youngster sniffed. "Mostly unasked and allus *unwanted.*"

"Us Counters're wanted every place we go, 'specially by the ladies," the blond giant corrected, as soberly as if he had taken the assertion seriously. "Only this uncle's not a Counter. His name's Front de Boeuf."

"That's a mighty impressive name," Dusty said, wondering if it was the information supplied by Mark which had caused the New Englander to let out a sharp breath and look disturbed. "But, what I've heard tell about them, I didn't figure the Front de Boeuf side of your kin to be cattlemen."

"The ones you're thinking about *aren't,*" Mark admitted with a wry grin. "Only Uncle Winston's not like Aunt Jessica and Cousin Tru'."

"Unless I've been told *wrong,* nobody's like *them,* or *shouldn't* be," the small Texan declared, aware that the pair of kinfolk named by the blond giant were notorious as the "black sheep" of the Front de Boeuf family.[1] However, being more concerned with the deteriorating relationship between his

1. *Information about some of the less than honest career of Jessica Front de Boeuf and her son, Trudeau, can be found in:* CUT ONE, THEY ALL BLEED *and Part Three, "Responsibility to Kinfolks,"* OLE DEVIL'S HANDS AND FEET; *also by inference, in: Part Two, "We Hang Horse Thieves High,"* J.T.'S HUNDREDTH.

companions and Sangster, while he hoped the light-hearted turn of the conversation might relieve the tension, he still decided he might have been given an excuse to separate them for a time and inquired, "You want to drop by and say, 'Howdy, you-all, Uncle Winston,' to him, *amigo*?"

"That'd be right pleasant, likely," the blond giant replied, guessing what had been the main motivation behind the offer. "Trouble being, I haven't seen him since I was a lil boy no more'n six foot high and don't have any notion where he's located, 'cepting it's north of the Platte somewheres."

"You wouldn't have run across him, would you, Ray?" Dusty inquired.

"*No!*" Sangster replied, with more vehemence than the question appeared to warrant. "In fact, according to the maps and information I've had, there's nothing but open land beyond where we'll be crossing the Platte. *Nobody* has *ever* taken title to any of it."

"Shucks, north of the Platte covers a whole heap of territory and Uncle Winston could be located 'most anywheres in it, and not even close to being right on the banks," Mark drawled, but he was prevented from continuing by their topping the rise and being brought into sight of their destination.

"Whooee!" Waco ejaculated, as the party drew rein and gazed at what was happening along a stretch of the level ground below. "So this's how they build a railroad?"

"Looks *easy*, don't it?" drawled the Kid.

"I *assure* you it's anything *but* that!" the New Englander stated with something close to asperity, his attitude suggesting he felt the remarks were intended to belittle his own efforts and problems.

"Lon only said's it *looks* easy, *Mr.* Sangster," Mark pointed out, visualizing the amount of organization which went into the seemingly uncomplicated work being carried out. "So does handling a trail herd. The *fun* starts when you try doing it."

"*This* isn't *fun!*" the New Englander snapped.

"Neither's handling three thousand or more longhorn on the trail, with the cash to keep you and your spread going riding on you getting 'em safe and well fed from Texas to the railroad, *mister*," Waco countered coldly. "They're some meaner'n your Eastern milk-cows and—!"

"There's something in that," Dusty put in, bringing the indignant tirade to a halt and wanting to avoid if possible a further worsening of the association between his companions and Sangster. Swinging from the saddle while speaking, the small Texan allowed the split-ended reins to slip from his grasp and "ground hitch" the well trained paint stallion. Then he went on, "I reckon both chores need plenty of thought to keep them going."

"Waco 'n' me'll 'tend to the hosses while you-all see what's to do, Dusty," the Kid suggested, having known why the small Texan had interrupted the youngster and, although in sympathy with him, sharing the belief that he and the New Englander should be kept apart as much as possible.

"*Gracias, amigo*," Dusty assented.

"I might's well come along," Mark asserted, considering he too had had all he could stand of Sangster's company for a while.

Squatting on his heels, with the New Englander doing the same by his side in a less effortless fashion, the small Texan started to study the scene in front of him. As far as he could see, the work force, mostly in their shirt sleeves and all having heavy boots of one kind or another on their feet, were comprised of a cross-section of European nationals. According to what he had been told by the New Englander, the majority were Irish, or of Celtic extraction. The rest had Anglo-Saxon, Germanic, Nordic, Latin, Grecian, East, West, or South Slavic features.[2] He had seen a number of them in Mulrooney and there were some with whom he had become acquainted in the line of duty as town marshal. A couple of young men clad in Eastern style riding clothes and less sturdy footwear were present, but not taking an active participation in

2. *"Slavic": of or pertaining to the Slavs—a branch of the Balto-Slavic subfamily of the Indo-European language family, consisting of three groups; "East," Russian, Ukranian, Ruthenian; "West," Czechoslovakian, Sorbian, Wendish, Polish, "South," Bulgarian, Serbo-Croatian, Slovenian.*

the work being carried out. Indicating them, Sangster said the shorter was Herbert Brill and the other Richard Reiser, fellow graduates of his college who he had brought with him to help supervise the construction.

Continuing to watch, Dusty was reminded of an anthill which had been disturbed. However, he soon realized—as was the case with ants apparently milling around aimlessly— there was a definite motive and concerted effort behind the way in which the large number of men working below carried out what at first appeared to be a jumble of intermingled and conflicting tasks. Despite the large number of workers involved, there was some justification for the comments about the apparent simplicity of the construction methods. It appeared to be a matter of keeping to a basic routine.

Beyond the point where the already laid rails ended, following white marker posts stretching in a straight line northwards, some of the men were digging a succession of shallow oblong holes at what were obviously preselected and evenly spaced distances apart. Another group, among whom Dusty identified the older of the Molloy brothers with whom he had been in contention at the Driven Spike Saloon, were placing thick wooden "sleepers" taken from the flat bed of a large horse-drawn wagon without sides, into the depressions. When one was tamped firmly with the earth which had been excavated, a task being carried out under the guidance of Louis "Frenchy" Rastignac, a sharp pointed and an "L"-shaped "spike" was placed on each end of it by an elderly man with a wheelbarrow containing a supply of them.

Nearer to where the small Texan was squatting, a section of the line was being laid and he gave the method employed his attention. Collecting a length of steel rail from one of the flat cars on the already laid track, Shamus O'Sullivan and four more gandy dancers of nearly his height carried it on their shoulders and set it down along the right side of the unoccupied sleepers just in front of the last portion to have been laid. Leading a similar team, Fritz "Dutchy" Voigt repeated the process on the left side. Although there were marks painted on the sleepers to indicate the relative positions of the two rails, a check of the "gauge" was made by Brill, using a device like an elongated and flattened lower case 'n' to ensure they were parallel and the exact required width apart.

When the young man was satisfied with his examination of the gauge, he made sure a small gap was left between the rails—to counteract the friction of wheels, or the heat of the sun, causing the metal to expand—before their ends were coupled together by "fish bolts" passing through holes in them and ther "fish-plates" which formed the bond. After nuts were tightened on the bolts, by the younger of the Molloy brothers at the right and a surly looking Slav on the left, a man used a slightly curved and metal tipped hand-spike—similar to those employed by sailors for changing the elevation or direction of a cannon on board a ship—to brace the sleeper. Then two more wielded sledge hammers, with the heads narrowing to blunted tips, to bury the spikes placed there ready for them into the wood until the bar of the "L" was hooked tightly over the base plate of the rail. By the time this was done, another two teams had delivered more lengths of rail and the sequence was repeated.

Studying the laying of the track for a few more minutes, Dusty decided the men all knew what they were doing. However, to his way of thinking, there was a lack of cohesion which made the work slower than necessary. This was particularly noticeable where the teams carrying the rails were concerned. Having set down the one they were delivering, they tended to get in the way of the next group while returning to the flat car. He also observed that Reiser did nothing to alleviate the situation.

"Well," Sangster said, straightening up with the air of considering enough time had been spent on watching the construction. "As I told you in Mulrooney, they could be working much *faster*."

"Likely," Dusty replied non-committally, also rising.

"Then when will you start *making* them do it?" the New Englander demanded rather than asked.

"*Me?*" the small Texan said. He was surprised that he had not been told of the two college graduates being in charge of the construction.

"I'm sorry, Dusty!" Sangster apologised, having detected a

note of asperity in the single word and having no desire to antagonize the man he felt sure would solve his problems. "I'm really worried about the slow rate we're moving and hope *you* can improve things."

"How about your two *amigos*?" Dusty queried.

"They are the surveyors, not gang bosses," the New Englander answered. "Which's probably the reason they can't make the men work faster. As I haven't anybody who can do that, I'm counting on *you* to do it."

CHAPTER TWELVE

They're a *Bad* Bunch

"Good evening to you, Cap'n Fog," Patrick Finnegan greeted in the booming tone which came so naturally to him that rumour around the railhead claimed he even whispered in a dull roar. However, unlike many people on first making the acquaintance of Dusty and Mark, he achieved the correct selection when confronted by the contrasting pair. "Sure and it's an honour to be welcoming you to my place, seeing's I never had a chance to meet you in Mulrooney. You'll be taking a drop of comfort with me, I'm hoping?"

"I'll be pleased and honoured, sir," Dusty Fog replied, accepting and shaking the massive right hand which retirement from being a gandy dancer had not softened to any noticeable degree. Having introduced his companions, he glanced around and went on, "You're busy tonight."

"There's little enough else for the boyos to be doing out here," Finnegan reminded, sounding just a trifle defensive. "And, with the little pay's they bring back from Mulrooney, 'tis few enough will have such bad heads they won't be able to do a day's work comes the morning."

Although Raymond Sangster had shown he did not approve of the decision, Dusty had declined to go to where the work on the spur-line was taking place and assume control immediately. He had grudgingly conceded the point that the small Texan wanted to make the acquaintance of the supervisory and non-manual employees—especially Herbert Brill and Richard Reiser—before doing so, in the hope of learning whether they had particular problems which could have contributed to the slow rate of progress. Nevertheless, Sangster had been uncommunicative on the ride back to the base camp and did nothing to improve the feelings of the other three Texans towards him. Nor did an incident on their arrival help matters. Mark Counter, the Ysabel Kid and Waco had once again offered to attend to Dusty's big paint stallion. It was a task he would normally have carried out personally, but he allowed them to help so that he could avoid the delay before meeting the men he had mentioned at the conclusion of his inspection. Prior to setting off with the small Texan, the unspoken assumption by the New Englander that *his* mount was also included in their offer had caused further annoyance to the three members of the OD Connected's floating outfit.

Going by appearances and his judgement of character, Dusty had concluded there was little wrong with the men to whom he was presented prior to the construction crew returning. All, from the operators of the telegraph service who allowed speedy communications to be maintained between the railhead and the outside world, to the accountant, struck him as being competent and sufficiently interested in their respective duties to be an asset rather than a liability. Renewing the acquaintance made in Mulrooney on the night of the abortive ambush, he was convinced that Doctor Brian Farnsworth would prove a tower of strength in whatever lay ahead. While far from being a soft touch willing to excuse men from working on the flimsiest excuse, the medical practitioner had considerable ability and a breezy "bedside manner" which made him popular and respected by the manual workers.

The accountant, Hubert Dayton, was a small man of fussy manner and a carefully maintained neat appearance. Clearly obsessed with the financial side of the construction, as soon as he was informed of the situation, he made a note of the arrangements Sangster had made to compensate Dusty for the time spent as gang boss. When he inquired how the other three Texans were to be listed for payment on the account ledger, Sangster had hinted they should be employed as assistants to the horse wranglers. Realizing how his *amigos*—and the blond youngster in particular—would respond to the suggestion, such work being assigned to those members of a ranch or trail drive crew who were unable for some reason to cope with handling the half wild longhorn cattle, Dusty had stated they would not require any financial remuneration from the railroad. Not only were they still on the payroll of the OD Connected ranch, but they had most of their earnings as deputy town marshals left, and Waco had shared out equally the not inconsiderable bounty Freddie Woods, as she still had been at the time, insisted he accepted from the issuing law enforcement agency for having brought to an end the career of the notorious outlaw, Richard "Tricky Dick" Cansole.[1]

On returning that evening, middle-sized stocky and harassed looking Herbert Brill had shown relief at being informed that he and his companion could return to their duties as surveyors. However, Richard Reiser had been less enamoured of the prospect. Tall and lean, his otherwise undistinguished sallow and hollow cheeked face had dull eyes and over-large lips set in something close to a sneer. Unlike the other surveyor, who had contrived to remain comparatively neat, his attire showed signs of grubbiness and a lack of attention beyond that merely caused by the day's work. He had snarled in a querulous tenor a demand to be told if his efforts were so unsatisfactory it was considered necessary to bring in an outsider to take his place. Nor had his attitude changed when told by Sangster this was not the case and he would be needed to continue the surveying of the route.

After having a meal in the large communal pavilion used as a mess-hall for the work crews, finding the food was cooked well and in adequate quantities, Dusty had elected to spend the evening getting to know and become known to such of the men he would be commanding who had not already made his acquaintance. He had known where the majority of them could be found and went there with his three *amigos*.

To the right of the work camp, and being by far the largest building—yet just as easy to dismantle and move onwards when necessary—was a canvas structure with a thin weatherboard frontage resembling that of a conventional saloon and announcing "FINNEGAN'S BAR AND GENERAL STORE. You Want It, We've Got It, Or Can Get It!". According to

---

1. *Told in*: THE MAKING OF A LAWMAN.

what Sangster had said when asked if the establishment could be a source of trouble leading to delay, its owner was a retired construction worker. Being allowed to conduct his business on account of a long standing friendship with Harland Todhunter, Patrick Finnegan did so with honesty and integrity. Because of the way he ran things, the New Englander had declared the drinks he had on sale in the bar-room were not responsible for the slow progress which had plagued the advance of the rails.

Remembering the building was constructed to be easily transportable, Dusty thought it was comfortably furnished and the bar had a good stock of various kinds of liquor—not just whiskey and beer—on its shelves. The score or so garishly dressed women mingling with the crowd were not likely to win any prizes for beauty and they lacked particularly good figures, but they were cheerful and far from being raddled old hags. All in all, despite the brief silence which descended when he and his companions came through the batwing doors of the main entrance, the friendly and relaxed atmosphere reminded him of that which prevailed in the saloons at Polveroso City when the crews of the local ranches were in town. Suspecting he was the subject of conversation when talking was resumed, he believed it would in general be favourable to him.

Looking around without making it obvious as he and his three *amigos* were accompanying the owner towards the bar, Dusty was not surprised to discover everybody present worked in some way for the railroad. Mostly they were construction hands of various kinds and unarmed, but he saw four men in dirty range clothes and wearing low tied guns as well as having knives hanging from their belts. Although beef was on the menu in the mess-hall that evening, they had been pointed out to him earlier by Raymond Sangster as the hunters employed to keep the work force supplied with meat from whatever kind of wild animals they could find.

However, as had been the case in the Driven Spike Saloon at Mulrooney on the day he had gone to confront the gandy dancers, the small Texan noticed that beer and not spirits was being consumed by the majority of the customers, and that the games of chance which were available attracted few players.

The meat hunters were drinking whiskey at a corner of the bar and, seated around a table in the centre of the room, half a dozen biggish men of Slavic appearance—including the one who had shared the task of tightening the nuts on the fish bolts with Stewart Molloy—had a bottle of some colourless liquor.

"You'll likely be joining the other high mucky-mucks in the backroom now, I reckon?" Finnegan queried, after having presented the Texans with the beers they requested and drunk to the success of the spur-line.

"Huh?" Dusty inquired.

"Mr. Sangster and the rest of the Pullman car crowd," the saloon-keeper elaborated, his tone giving only the slightest hint of his disapproval for the men to whom he was referring. "They wouldn't be coming out front here with the work crews."

"Here'll do us just fine," the small Texan declared and knew he had won a point in Finnegan's estimation. "Fact being, I'm figuring on going around to get to know those of them I haven't already met."

"Is there *anything* I can do for you first?" the saloon-keeper inquired.

"Tell me what you reckon's making the work go so slow," Dusty requested, concluding this was part of the advice he was expected to seek and giving a signal his companions interpreted correctly as asking them to make sure the conversation was not overheard by the other occupants of the room. Waiting until they spread along the counter on either side of himself and the owner, he continued, "If it is going slow."

"It *is*," Finnegan confirmed, nodding his approval at Dusty's caution and discrediting the rumour of his loud voice for once by holding his tone at a level which carried only to the small Texan. "But that's not the fault of the work crews. They're good men and hard working, *most* of 'em."

"Then who is to blame?" Dusty inquired, making a mental note of the emphasis placed on the word "*most*," and concluding the point would be elaborated if he asked.

"It starts at the *top*," the saloon-keeper assessed. "Not with Harl' Todhunter, though. He might be a lousy poker player and likes *Scotch* whisky—as them *Scotch* Jaspers call it—but he sure as hell knows how to get a railroad built. It's that college-boy New Englander he's put in charge. That one doesn't know sic 'em about handling men and those he's brought to help him're no better at it."

"Brill and Reiser?"

"Brill's all right at his own line of work by all accounts and he doesn't get underfoot too much while he's checking the gauge, which's all he does when he's not surveying ahead."

"And Reiser?"

"No matter what kind of surveyor he is—and he claims to have found a real good place to cross the Platte—Reiser doesn't strike me's being any use at all up at the railhead," Finnegan answered. "Tries real *hard* to be *popular*. He keeps on letting on he's all for the 'workers,' happen you know what I mean. Top of which, he plays *favourites,* from what I've heard, and that *never* goes down well with gandy dancers."

"There's nothing wrong with showing a few favours to good men," Dusty commented, feeling sure such were not selected. "It helps make the others try harder."

"His favourites aren't the *good* men and having anybody follow *their* lead wouldn't help *speed up* the track-laying," the saloon-keeper replied, confirming the small Texan's supposition. "It's mostly those Russians over there watching us so careful. Happen you don't reckon it's too forward of me, Cap'n, I'd keep *both* eyes on 'em was I you. They're a *bad* bunch. What I've seen of 'em and the way I've heard 'em talking after they been drinking that vodka stuff they've had me get 'special for 'em, I'd've thought they'd be off some place planning a revolution, 'stead of raising what bit of sweat they raise helping build the spur-line."

"Are they causing fuss?" Dusty asked, looking at the men he had noticed drinking the colourless liquid.

"Nothing more than belly-aching about the food and how *everybody's* expected to work too hard for too little pay."

"If it's always like the meal we had tonight, I wouldn't say there's anything wrong with the food."

"It's allus the same. Old Manny Bone's a damned good cook and sees to that."

"And the work?"

"It's as well paid as any other railroad gives and, being on this sort of country instead of going up and down damned great hills like some do, the work's easier if anything. Leastwise, that's how the gandy dancers's matter see it."

"Meaning Shamus O'Sullivan, Frenchy Rastignac and Dutchy Voigt?" Dusty guessed.

"Them in particular," Finnegan confirmed. "And, what they say and do, the rest're likely to listen and follow. I hear tell your trails have crossed down to Mulrooney?"

"We come 'round to seeing things eye to eye," the small Texan admitted with a grin, having no doubt the trio had told of their experiences and feeling just as sure he had come out of the descriptions in a satisfactory fashion. "I locked horns with a couple more of 'em the last time they were in."

"The Molloy boys?" the saloon-keeper named, glancing to where the brothers were sharing a table with the trio just mentioned. "I don't reckon you'll have no trouble with *them*. Fact being, all Bob and Stewart's been asking is, 'How the hell did we figure Cap'n Fog was *little*?' That and saying they don't intend to get that drunk again when you're around." He paused before going on with a grin, "Anyways, you'll soon know how they feel about things. They're coming over here and I don't reckon it's just to buy drinks for themselves 'cause they're too tight-fisted to call in a round."

"Howdy, Cap'n Fog," the older brother greeted in an amiable fashion. "Can't bring to mind *much* about it myself, but Shamus tells us's how we *met* you in the Driven Spike."

"I believe we had that *honour*," Dusty admitted, also smiling.

"Then I hopes's how there's no ill feelings," Stewart said and his sibling nodded concurrence.

"Not on my part, any more than on yours," the small Texan confirmed.

"Would you be coming over and joining us for a spell, Cap'n?" Bob suggested.

"It'll be my pleasure," Dusty assented and looked at the saloon-keeper. "Happen you'll excuse me, Mr. Finnegan?"

"I reckon we'll go over and see happen we can win some at

blackjack, Dusty," Mark said, after the burly owner had signified agreement. "We feel lucky and this could be our night to
howl."

"*Bueno*!" the small Texan drawled, knowing why the comment was made. His companions were aware, as had been the
case at the Driven Spike Saloon, that he wished to avoid any
suggestion that he was depending upon them for backing.
"Don't *win* too much."

"Was I one of them heathen *Scotch* Jaspers's don't know
the proper way to spell 'whiskey' with an 'e,' like it should
be," Finnegan put in cheerfully. "I'd say, 'Don't *win* at all.'
But as I'm not, good luck to you."

"Just look who is here, comrades," requested the Slavic-
looking man who had been tightening the nuts on the fish-
plates, speaking in a carrying tone, as Dusty was walking with
the brothers back to their table. He was seated with his legs
clear of the table, but had his hands hidden underneath. "It's
the hired killer who Sangster has brought to drive us to work
with his guns."

"There's no call for *that*, Krushchev!" Bob Molloy declared coldly, starting to move forward.

"*Easy!*" Dusty commanded, catching the Irishman by the
right arm and bringing him to a halt before he could complete
the first step. "This's between me and him." Then, looking at
the burly and hard faced Russian, he continued in a soft voice
which held the chill and menace of a Texan blue norther
storm's first whisper, "You've got something on your mind,
hombre, so get it said."

"I don't like hired gun hands being brought to force honest
men to work like slaves," Ivan Krushchev stated, his words
slurred as if he was well on the way to being drunk, still
keeping his hands concealed beneath the level of the table.
"*That* is what's on my mind!"

"These guns of mine seem to worry you," the small Texan
drawled and his hands crossed in a close to sight-defying-blur
to fetch the Colt 1860 Army Model revolvers from their holsters. There was a concerted gasp from the onlookers and an
expression of alarm came to the Russian's unprepossessing
face. However, instead of the hammers being cocked, they

were twirled and offered butt first to the older brother. "Would you hold these for me, *amigo*, so's I can see what kind of a difference they make?"

"S—Sure, Cap'n Fog," Bob assented, accepting the weapons.

"There you are, *loud mouth*!" Dusty said, moving clear of the brothers and spreading his hands well clear of his sides. "I don't have my guns any more!"

Letting out a profanity in his native tongue, Krushchev thrust himself from his chair with a speed which implied the apparent drunkenness was only a pretence. While not the largest of his party, he still had a considerable advantage in height and weight over the small Texan. However, he was not intending to rely upon this for the attack he was launching. Instead, he was grasping a broken glass beer mug by its handle and thrust its jagged edges at Dusty's face.

CHAPTER THIRTEEN

We'll Be Doing Things My Way

Exclamations of alarm, some registering anger arose from almost everybody in the bar-room, the loudest of the latter coming from its owner. However, even as Patrick Finnegan moved forward and the men who had been drinking with the Molloy brothers came to their feet, the need for intervention was brought to an end.

Alert for whatever kind of attack might be launched, Dusty Fog's mind reacted at lightning speed to come up with the defence best suited to his needs. Responding with the speed he had displayed when drawing his Colt 1860 Army Model revolvers a few seconds earlier, his right hand swung towards his attacker. The two forearms met mid-way between their bodies to deflect the jagged edges of the glass off target and opening Ivan Krushchev's guard for what came next. As had happened when dealing with the Molloy brothers in Mulrooney, the blow struck by the small Texan was not delivered in what his audience would have considered to be a conventional fashion. Coming up behind a stiff, locked wrist, his unclenched left hand travelled at most two feet before making contact. However, arriving with fingers spread slightly to offer rigidity, the heel of his palm caught the Russian's chin with considerable force. Lifted on to his tiptoes, the broken beer mug slipping from his suddenly inoperative grasp, he staggered backwards a couple of paces like a pole-axed steer before sprawling supine on the floor.

For a moment, a number silence dropped over the entire room. With the exception of the other Texans, nobody—not even those gandy dancers who had seen the small Texan in

111

bare-handed action at Mulrooney on various occasions—could imagine exactly what had happened. Then an excited chatter welled up as the spectators tried to work out exactly how Krushchev had been dropped like a log before his attack could be completed. However, no such discussion was carried out by his five companions. Instead, they started to rise so quickly that a couple of them overturned their chairs.

"If any more'n just *one* of you Ruskie spalpeens tries to take it up for Krushchev!" Shamus O'Sullivan thundered, his voice carrying above every other in a menacing fashion. "It's me you'll be up again' as well's Cap'n Fog!"

The burly Irish gandy dancer did not advance alone!

"And *me* too, *m'sieurs*!" Louis "Frenchy" Rastignac supplemented from O'Sullivan's right side.

"You can count *me* in on it with Shamus and Frenchie!" asserted Fritz 'Dutchy' Voigt, at the Irishman's left.

Glancing around, knowing the trio's ability in a roughhouse brawl individually or as a team, all but one of the Russians stood still. However, the exception was the largest of them. Black bearded and massive, Rudolph Gorbachov's looks and, at that moment, demeanour explained his nickname, "the Bear". Snarling words which were practically incoherent to even his companions, he lurched towards the small Texan. Except that, as others had discovered under similar circumstances, he suddenly found Dusty no longer appeared small. Rather Gorbachov had the sensation of being confronted by a man whose bulk and height exceeded his own. Being dull witted and superstitious, such a phenomenon produced an unnerving effect. However, it did not cause him to halt his advance or lower his outstretched huge hands. Which proved unfortunate.

Although Dusty had dealt with his first attacker barehanded, he was disinclined to employ such tactics against the much larger second, who he felt sure did not share his predecessor's belief that he would be taken unawares. Not that he gave a thought to retrieving his guns from Bob Molloy. He carried a more primitive and simple weapon readily available and was confident it would fill his needs just as effectively under the circumstances. In fact, despite the move having gone unnoticed by anybody apart from the other three members of the OD Connected's floating outfit—who were watching without moving closer—he was already bringing it from the right back pocket of his Levi's pants. What was more, when removed, it was so small that it remained unobserved.

The device appeared to be nothing more dangerous than a piece of a broom's handle about six inches in length. However, it was made of Osage orange—the *bois d'arc* tree regarded by Indian bow makers as being the finest, hardest and most durable of woods—and, in addition to the ends being rounded, there were half a dozen grooves encircling its centre to serve as a hand-grip. Although Dusty's *amigos* were more knowledgeable, he doubted whether anybody else in the barroom would have identified it as a *yawara* stick such as was first developed and used on the Pacific island of Okinawa. Nor were they aware that he had learned how to wield it from the man who taught him the unusual, yet more efficacious, bare-hand fighting techniques he had employed.

Instead of taking what most of the people present considered to be the advisable precaution of backing away from "the Bear," Dusty lunged to meet him. Already startled by the metamorphosis which seemed to have come over his proposed victim, Gorbachov's never nimble wits failed to cope with the latest and most unexpected development. He had grown accustomed to antagonists showing more discretion when faced by his charge and could not think quickly enough to decide how to deal with one who failed to do so. Nor was he granted any opportunity to decide upon a line of action. Before he realized fully what was happening, the *big* Texan was passing between his reaching hands. Not that he was permitted to clamp them home as he had intended.

Driven forward with all Dusty's strength and skill, the rounded end of the *yawara* stick emerging from between his right thumb and forefinger struck the inverted "U" shaped cavity below the centre of the huge Russian's rib cage. Never had he known such pain. It numbed his whole body, even automotive functions like breathing being affected. Not only was his advance brought to an immediate halt and all the air expelled from his lungs, the agony caused him to retreat. However, the response was involuntary. Losing consciousness before he had taken two steps, his legs became entangled and he crashed backwards on to the table he and his companions had been using. Breaking under his weight, sending glasses and the half empty bottle to shatter and spray their contents over the hard packed dirt floor, it deposited him supine and helpless amongst wreckage.

"Does anybody else of you-all want some?" the small Texan inquired of the remaining Russians, still speaking in a soft and yet chilling fashion. He was standing in the half crouching posture which his uncle, General Jackson Baines "Ole Devil" Hardin's Japanese valet, Tommy Okasi, had taught him was most suited for using either the *yawara* stick of the *ju-jitsu* and *karate* techniques he had often found just as efficacious. [1] However, because of the strength of his personality, it did not make him look any smaller to the obviously startled men he was addressing. "If so, come ahead and we'll get her done!"

As had been the case with the two men lying on the floor, the other four Russians had a decided advantage in size and weight over Dusty. However, affected by the sense of potency he exuded, they were mutually discinclined to take up the challenge of the *big* Texan who had felled their companions with such apparent ease.

"Ivan is always troublesome when he's been drinking," the smallest of the quartet claimed and, having been watching him for guidance, his companions muttered concurrence. While no cleaner or prepossessing than the rest, he spoke in the manner of one who had had a good education. "And Rudolph is *his* friend, so must have felt he must be avenged."

"Like I said, how do *you-all* feel on it?" Dusty demanded, without relaxing his vigilance or mentioning certain points about the attack which were puzzling him and, he felt, required investigation.

"Things were said which should not have been," Pavel

1. *Information about the connection between Dusty Fog and Tommy Okasi is given in*: APPENDIX ONE.

Gorki answered quietly and in a tone lacking conviction, continuing to act as spokesman for the group.

"Your *amigo* talked *louder* than that," Dusty said pointedly and gestured around him. "And I reckon, seeing's you've got up, everybody who heard him would like to know how the rest of you feel about me being here."

"Rudolph should not have said what he did," Gorki announced in a more carrying—albeit disgruntled and grudging —voice and, under the impulsion of the *big* Texan's cold gaze, his companions made similar declarations.

"Then it's *over* and done with," Dusty stated, returning the *yawara* stick to his back pocket without any of the railroad workers or the saloon's employees having noticed it. Accepting the Colts from Bob Molloy and replacing them in their holsters, he gestured towards the motionless figures and continued, "You'd best get your *amigos* to their beds and have Doctor Farnsworth take a look at them."

"And don't *any* of you be coming back this night," Patrick Finnegan added, having strode up bristling with anger. " 'Tis knowing you should be that I'll not be having trouble caused in my place."

"When'll you be taking over as gang boss, Cap'n Fog, sir?" O'Sullivan asked, strolling over with his two companions while the four Russians were starting to carry out Dusty's order.

"Comes morning," the small Texan replied, conscious of having everybody in the room listening to his words. He was also confident that the incident had impressed even those of the gandy dancers who had seen him in action at Mulrooney, when a breach of the peace called for him to act against some of their number. He believed what had happened would make them more willing to go along with the measures he intended to instigate. "And, while I can't say's how I've ever done any railroad building like you-all have, we'll be doing things *my* way."

"Howdy, Ray," Dusty Fog said, descending from the flat car of the train near where the New Englander was standing, obviously awaiting its arrival. He and the work force had returned to the base camp on it at the end of the fifth day since he had taken over as gang boss. "We're still moving along pretty well, wouldn't you say, Bert?"

"Very well indeed," Herbert Brill confirmed, showing satisfaction both at the use of the abbreviated version of his Christian name and at being asked for an opinion by a man he had come greatly to admire.

As the small Texan had envisaged, the way he had dealt with the Russians gave him a moral ascendancy which enabled him to put in hand the changes in routine he had planned more easily than might otherwise have been the case. Even before the two unconscious would-be assailants were removed by their companions, the rest of the railroad workers were showing they approved of his actions and they listened with interest to what he had to say about his intentions. Such was the impact he had made that, when it was learned Ivan Krushchev and Rudolph Gorbachov were so badly injured Doctor Brian Farnsworth had ordered them sent back to Mulrooney on the supply train, the general concensus of opinion had been they had asked for all they received.

The fact that Krushchev had only pretended to be drunk and was holding the glass beer mug, which must have been broken earlier ready for use as a weapon, suggested to the small Texan it had been planned for use at the first opportunity. What was more, the rest of the Russians must have known at least something of his intentions. The supposition had been given strength by Waco, who possessed a flair for deductive reasoning which he had found useful as a peace officer, and who examined the broken bottle. Although most of its contents had been sprayed over the floor when it was shattered, there was just sufficient remaining in the bottom for him to be able to tell it had held water and not the potent vodka they usually drank. Being told of this, Finnegan questioned his employees and discovered none of them had sold the bottle to the party. However, the other four had given no further trouble and the pressure of his duties had prevented Dusty from looking deeper into the reason for the attack. Nor, wanting to avoid possible friction, would be allow the blond youngster to do so. Not that the quartet were around long enough for him to feel any particular concern over their presence.

Although Brill had become a willing assistant, Richard Reiser had refused to even go out to the work site. In fact, he had left the base camp on the morning after the incident and, claiming he had learned of family problems, sent his resignation by telegraph from Mulrooney. Next day, when the news was circulated, the Russians had asked for their pay and quit. Despite the departures arousing speculation amongst the Texans, neither the quartet nor the surveyor were missed. This was especially true of Reiser, who had sexual proclivities the vast majority of the gandy dancers considered abhorrent. In fact, according to rumour, the six Russians were the only ones who did not share the general disgust.[2]

First and most important of the small Texan's changes to

2. A subsequent investigation by Deputy United States' Marshal Solomon Wisdom "Solly" Cole established that, being of "liberal" persuasions, Richard Reiser had been collaborating with the Russians—who were anarchists as Patrick Finnegan had suggested—in trying to disrupt the construction work. Being disinclined to take any more chances than were absolutely necessary, it was decided their efforts would only be on a minor scale until they had crossed the Platte River and were further away from any law enforcement agency which might be called upon to look into their activities. However, sensing Dusty Fog would prove a serious deterrent to their intentions, Reiser had insisted he must be removed and suggested a plan for doing so. It had required the promise of a fair sum of money before a volunteer was procured to carry out the scheme and much persuasion before the others would agree to taking a bottle containing water instead of vodka with them to drink while simulating intoxication as an "excuse" for the attack. Pressed by them for the payment he had promised, despite the ploy having failed, and having so little faith in their reliability and integrity that he believed his part in the affair would be disclosed to the big Texan, when no payment was forthcoming, Reiser had concluded the safest course was flight. Learning he would not be returning and fearing he would betray them, being equally distrustful of him and one another by nature, they had followed his example by taking their departure.

2a. *Some details of the career as a peace officer of Solomon Wisdom "Solly" Cole can be found in*: IS-A-Man; Part one, "To Separate Innocence from Guilt," MORE J.T.'S LADIES; DECISION FOR DUSTY FOG; CALAMITY SPELLS TROUBLE *and Part Six, "Mrs. Wild Bill,"* J.T.'s LADIES.

the method of laying the track was that the teams carrying the pieces of rail returned to the flat car to collect their next rail by walking parallel and a few feet clear of either the left or right side of the line, depending upon which they were working, instead of returning close along it and getting in the way of those who were coming with the next portion to be laid. On putting this into practice, with control of the teams delegated to the men who he had estimated were best capable of exerting it, they had found the whole process went more smoothly. He had also instigated having all the equipment checked before leaving the base camp in the morning and, by doing so, ended the delays he was told by Frenchy Rastignac had often oc- curred because it was discovered on arrival at the work area that items required for use had been forgotten.

However, the most important change wrought by Dusty arose from the way he handled the construction crew. Pos- sessed of an inborn flair for leadership, which had been im- proved by his years in command of Company 'C' of the Texas Light Cavalry during the War Between the States and as *se- gundo* of the OD Connected ranch—one of the largest in Texas—he had the ability to inspire confidence and produce a willingness to carry out his wishes which were never achieved by Reiser. Therefore, by leading rather than driving—as some men would have tried to do—he caused more track to be laid each day than had previously been the case.

"It will have to be even *better*," Raymond Sangster as- serted, waving the buff coloured telegraph message form he was carrying. "Mr. Todhunter is bringing those Englishmen from the Railroad Commission in three days, so they can see how well we are doing. You'll have to make the men work even *faster*, Dusty. How much track can you have them laying from tomorrow?"

"They won't be laying *any* track tomorrow," the small Texan replied, thinking of something he had been considering since he took over as gang boss. "Nor the next day at least, comes to that."

"Y—You can't be *serious!*" the New Englander gasped, staring in consternation and Brill showed an equal surprise.

"I've never been *more* serious in my life," Dusty declared and there was a timbre of refusing to brook any objections in his voice as he continued, "There'll be no more track laid for two days!"

CHAPTER FOURTEEN

Slow-elking's the Same's
Stealing Cattle

"Well, Sir John, gents," Harland Todhunter said, watching the work being carried out on the spur-line in the company of three other members of the Railroad Commission. "What do you think about the way things are going?"

"It's most impressive!" Sir John Uglow Ramage replied.

"They are working *much* faster than I've seen it being done on the railroad in Canada," Jean Pierre Radisson commented.

"Are those chaps of yours *always* moving at this speed, Dusty?" Lord James Roxton inquired, as the small Texan came up the slope upon which the party was standing.[1]

"I'd have to say 'no' to that," Dusty Fog admitted. "Fact being, the boys've been known to slow down a mite on occasion."

Overhearing the comments while approaching, Dusty was pleased by the proof that his insistence upon doing no construction for the two preceding days was justified!

Waiting until Raymond Sangster had spluttered into indignant silence, the small Texan had explained his decision. Although he had been satisfied with the way in which the construction crews were working, he had noticed there were often delays where one very important task was concerned.

1. *Space does not permit us to go into detail about the appearance of the four members of the Railroad Commission. However, their descriptions and information about some of their activities since reaching Mulrooney are given in*: DECISION FOR DUSTY FOG *and* DIAMONDS, EMERALDS, CARDS AND COLTS.

They were only brief individually, but added up to time lost in the aggregate. Because of the—deliberately it was proved later—insufficient precautions taken by the Russians who Richard Reiser had assigned to the duty, many of the fish-bolts had been left uncovered out of doors and regardless of the weather, and had become so rusty they could only be forced through the holes in the equally neglected fish-plates and rails with difficulty. Securing them with the nuts was no easier.

Instead of taking the construction hands to where they had ceased laying track the previous day, Dusty had put them to work cleaning and greasing the nuts, bolts and holes in the rails and fish-plates. Because of his knowledge of how to handle men he had explained why he wanted the tedious and dirty work carried out, although this would not have occurred to either Sangster or his predecessor as gang boss. Learning what he had in mind and finding it amusing, as well as seeing the point, the gandy dancers had set about the task with a willingness and cheerfulness which would have been absent if they had been ordered to do it without the explanation. What was more, he had prevailed upon the New Englander to ensure there were sufficient barrels of beer obtained—including a couple supplied free by Patrick Finnegan—to quench the men's thirsts over the two days required to complete the work without leading to skimping of the cleaning due to intoxication.

How effective the precaution had been was proved when Todhunter arrived with the two Englishmen and the French-Canadian to carry out the inspection. They had reached the construction area about two hours after work was commenced. Taking in the sight, even the American member of the Railroad Commission—with his much greater knowledge of how the laying of rails was performed—was impressed by what was to be seen. Such was the determination displayed by the gandy dancers to put on a good show for the visitors, they threw themselves into the task with vim and vigour in excess of anything previously exhibited. In fact, Dusty had had to curb some of their enthusiasm when it threatened to disrupt the smooth and rapid flow of the various inter-connected activities from their correct sequence. Despite this, they had laid close to a mile of track at a rate of progress which Todhunter considered must have been a record time. Before asking the others if they were satisfied with what they could see, he had signalled for the small Texan to join them.

"Have you run into any difficulties?" Ramage inquired.

"None worth mentioning," Dusty claimed, considering the incident with the Russians to be a personal matter which had not delayed construction.

"How about when you get to the Platte River?" Radisson wanted to know. "Will crossing it create problems?"

"Not according to the report I've been told one of the surveyors turned in," the small Texan replied.

"Which one?" Todhunter asked.

"Mr. Reiser, afore he had to quit because of some trouble in his family," Dusty supplied, successfully concealing his disenchantment with the man in question. "He allowed's how he'd found a bridge the Army's Corps of Engineers've put across and it'll stand up to letting work trains go over until something even stronger's built. I haven't seen it yet, mind, so I can't say more than that until I have, and heard what Bert Brill reckons."

"Young Reiser's a good surveyor, gents," Todhunter claimed. "If he's satisfied, everything'll be all right." He glanced apologetically at the small Texan and went on, "Not that I blame you for wanting a second opinion, Captain Fog."

"*Gracias*," Dusty drawled non-committally. "Are *you* satisfied with the way things are going, Mr. Todhunter?"

"You bet your life I am," the railroad magnate confirmed and the suggestion that he was impressed by what he had seen was genuine. "I'm real grateful to you for coming and helping Raymond Sangster out."

"I owe him a favour," Dusty said quietly.

"Will you be coming all the way to Canada, Captain Fog?" Radisson wanted to know.

"Nope," Dusty denied. "I'm just giving Ray a hand until he can get another gang boss."

"Will finding one cause any difficulties, Harland?" Ramage queried.

"None that can't be got over," Todhunter asserted with

confidence. "There're a few around who've worked for me before and, knowing how things stand with Captain Fog, I've already sent for one of them to come and take over from him. Anyways, if you've seen enough, we might's well be headed back to the base camp."

"I'd like to see the work at close hand," Ramage hinted and the other two non-American visitors added their support.

"Come on down then," Todhunter assented, being just as interested in discovering how the high rate of progress was achieved. After the examination at close range was concluded, without the secret having been detected by the other delegates as far as he could determine and when they had stated their willingness to return to the base camp, he said, "If you reckon the work crews can manage without you, I'd like you to come along with us, Captain Fog. There's some champagne and a better meal than you've likely had for a spell waiting for you to share with us."

"I reckon they can manage just fine," the small Texan claimed with confidence. "I've got some good men handling things and they'll keep the track moving just as well whether I'm here or not."

"Then we'll leave them to it and head back," Todhunter stated. Raising his voice, he addressed the men who were continuing with their various tasks. "There'll be free drinks for all of you in Finnegan's tonight, boys. By god, you've *earned* them."

"This here's a *no account* way of spending time," Waco complained in something close to petulance, throwing away the handful of straw with which he had been massaging the back of his big paint stallion and looking around the base camp with disfavour. "I've done so much grooming, I'll be wearing my ole Dusty hoss down to a nubbin."

"I seem to mind you reckoning you was having to work too hard when we was running the law back to Mulrooney," Mark Counter commented dryly, despite sharing the sentiment, from where he was performing a similar task with his bloodbay stallion. "Now you don't like having *nothing* to do all day."

"*Walk* too hard, not *work*," the blond youngster corrected.

"That's the whole damned trouble with hereabouts. There isn't *nothing* for us to do."

Apart from Dusty Fog, none of the OD Connected's floating outfit was involved in any way with the construction of the spur-line. Nor, aware it was still necessary for him to be seen as having no need for their backing in anything he did, could the other three take a more active interest. They had been out to the area where the tracks were being laid on a couple of occasions. However, except for the blond giant having entertained the rest of the gandy dancers during a rest period by just he and Shamus O'Sullivan carrying three rails in succession from the flat car to the unoccupied sleepers, they had been there solely in the capacity of visitors.

Being vigorous by nature, Waco was finding time hanging heavily on his hands and had become bored with the inactivity even more quickly than the other two. Nor had the period since he had joined the floating outfit been any inducement for him to accept the present situation. He had never felt such tedium while working as a deputy town marshal. Each day had brought something new to demand his attention. Even what leisure he had had was spent in an interesting fashion, learning a variety of things he would put to good use later in life.

"Why don't we go hunting for a spell?" the Ysabel Kid inquired, being in accord with his two *amigos* over the boring state of affairs. "I'm getting tired of eating nothing but beef."

"Hey, that's *right*!" Waco ejaculated, the instincts acquired while a peace officer stirring. They presented a suggestion he felt worth acting upon, but more from a sense of justice than out of boredom. "Those four jasper's're hired for hunting haven't brought in no elk, deer, pronghorn, nor even bear since we got here, only *beef*."

"Which folks raise beef hereabouts," Mark pointed out, although he guessed what the youngster was thinking.

"They can't have very good roundups, happen they let so many go uncaught for branding," Waco countered, thinking of the number of cattle which must have been delivered to the cook ever since their arrival at the base camp. "What say we sort of drift over and take a look at those meat-hunting yahoos' camp?"

"It'll be *something* to do," Mark admitted, his tone giving no indication of how seriously he regarded the possibilities which prompted the suggestion.

"Hell, yes," the Kid drawled, so laconically he too might have been doing no more than seekin something to break the monotony. "It should do *that*."

"Could drop by the cookshack on the way there," Waco hinted.

"You know," Emanuel "Manny" Bone said, when the three Texans arrived at the kitchen and Waco asked about the supplying of meat. "I never give it a thought, but they've *never* brought in anything 'cepting beef."

"How'd they bring it?" the youngster inquired. "I mean, who does the butchering?"

"That's something else I hadn't thought on 'til now," the big and jovial featured cook admitted, losing his usual cheerful expression. "Every other bunch I've had bringing meat left me to get it skinned and butchered. This bunch've always hauled it in already dressed."

"Let's go take a look at their camp," Mark said grimly.

"I'll come with you," Bone announced.

"There's *some* might say's how we wouldn't have no legal juris—whatever the god-damned word is—up here, even was we still wearing badges in Mulrooney," the Kid remarked as the party set off to conduct the investigation.

"We can allus make a citizen's arrest," Waco pointed out mildly. "Should it be *needed*."

The meat hunters had set up their camp a short distance away from the rest of the structures. It was not a salubrious sight. There were a couple of grubby looking tents and, its team and their saddle horses being tethered nearby, the covered wagon they used for their work served as something of a windbreak. None of them were in view, so the Texans and the cook went towards half a dozen barrels and a pile of hides alongside the smaller tent.

"They take the tallow 'n' skins for themselves," Bone remarked. "And, seeing's how the railroad don't have no need for either, there's been no arguments."

"You bunch want *something*?" inquired a harsh and hostile voice, before anything more could be said.

Followed by the other three and Raymond Sangster—who looked as if he found their company as repugnant as he did that of anybody else he considered beneath his social station —Michael Buerk, the lanky leader of the meat hunters emerged from the larger tent before the Texans and Bone could reach the others.

"How come you fellers're bringing in *beef* all the time instead of wild critter?" Waco asked, without giving a direct answer.

"I don't see's how its any of your never-mind," Buerk replied in a surly fashion and flickered a glance suggestive of worry at the two Texans and the cook as they came to a halt in a half circle behind the youngster. "But it's 'cause there ain't enough wild critters 'round hereabouts to do the feeding."

"What's wrong with *beef*?" Sangster challenged, without noticing the way in which the other three hunters were matching their leader's reaction and moving into a line on either side of him.

"That depends on who-all's beef it is," Waco replied.

"As *nobody* has legal title to the land across the Platte where these gentlemen are hunting," the New Englander said, with the air of stating the obvious except that it was underlaid with a worried timbre, "any cattle there must be running wild."

"We don't keep 'em penned up on the lower forty like Eastern milk cows, *mister*," the blond youngster countered. "And longhorns roam plenty, but whoever puts a brand on 'em owns 'em, no matter where they go."

"And have those brought in by Mr. Buerk and his men brands on them?" Sangster asked.

"There's a *real* easy way of finding out," Waco replied. "We'll go take us a look."

"Like hell you will!" Buerk snarled, having no desire for the examination to be made. The matter was taken from his hands in no uncertain fashion as he continued, "You're not wearing bad—!"

Thinking he was not observed, the man on the far left of the hunters grabbed for his Colt. Instantly, he discovered he had made an error. Alert to the possibility, none of the Texans were giving their full attention to Buerk and Sangster. They were aware that the suggested inspection would be more than just resented by the hunters. Anywhere in cattle country, because the half wild longhorn cattle were allowed to fend for themselves on the open range and often wandered for considerable distances, the right of ownership being established by the brand on the animal was considered inviolate. Therefore, to have killed cattle which were so identified classed as theft and was treated by drastic methods when discovered.

The moment their owners saw the hostile gesture, five hands moved immediately. Four descended in the conventional fashion, but the other had its palm turned outwards. While thumbs coiled over hammer spurs, the fingers coiled around the butts of the revolvers waiting in holsters and the draws were commenced with slight variations of speed. Fastest of all, Mark's two ivory handled 1860 Army Colts cleared leather. An instant later, the staghorn butted brace owned by Waco came out and the one on the right thundered. Twisted free in the manner required due to being carried with the walnut grips pointing forward, the single big old Dragoon Colt was brought into alignment by the Kid. However, the latter movement was only just completed as the youngster's bullet took the man who had started to draw in the right shoulder and spun him sideways with his weapons not yet quite fully drawn.

Watching the speed with which the first two Texans in particular armed themselves, the hammers of the unfired Colts also being taken to fully cocked although not released as the barrels were pointing forward, Buerk and the other hunters restrained the movements their hands were making towards their guns. If they had not been aware of the reputation acquired by Mark and the Kid, even before becoming peace officers in Mulrooney, as well as having heard of Waco's capability as a gun fighter whilst a deputy town Marshal, the way they had found themselves looking into the muzzles of the Colts would have served as a warning that they were up against men extremely well versed in all matters *pistolero* and could in all probability back up the rapidity with accurately placed lead. The latter point received verification from the fate which had befallen their companion.

Yet, although none of the hunters realized it, the one who was shot might have counted himself fortunate. He had been hit in the shoulder and it would be some considerable time before he could regain the use of the right hand, but he had suffered nothing worse. That would not have been the case before Waco had met Dusty Fog and the other members of the floating outfit. In those days, he would have shot to kill without hesitation or giving the matter a second thought. Because of the change wrought upon him by association with the small Texan in particular, he now dealt with each situation according to its merits and, this time, had realized there was no need for him to take such extreme measures. What was more, aware the cook and Sangster would be endangered if a fight commenced, he had sufficient confidence in his ability to fire and just inflict an injury which would prevent the hunter from starting gun play liable to involve everybody else.

"Let's have those hands raised a whole heap higher!" Mark commanded and the three uninjured hunters complied with alacrity.

"Just what do you think you're *doing*?" Sangster demanded, his face pallid and his demeanour showing he was shaken by what had happened. "You *can't*—!"

"We can," Waco corrected, thumb cocking the right hand Colt deftly. "And *have*!"

"By what *right*—?" the New Englander began.

"You'll know when we've took a look at them hides," the youngster stated. "If they've got brands on 'em, these *hombres*'ve been shooting and selling somebody's stock to the railroad."

"It's called 'slow-elking' back home to Texas," the Kid elaborated, looking at his most Comanche. "And slow-elking's the same's stealing cattle. Which's a *crime* against the legal law, *Mister* Sangster, and a man don't need no peace officer's badge to stop *anybody* breaking it."

"You don't *know* they've broken the law!" the New Englander protested, his antipathy towards the Texans causing him to utter protests he felt at the bottom of his heart were unjustified.

"Then let's go and find out," Mark suggested. "You reckon you can keep those jaspers *amused* while we're doing it, Lon?"

"I'll lend a hand, happen you can't, Kid," Bone offered, going to collect the revolver which had fallen from the wounded man's holster as he spun around.

"They're branded all right," Mark declared, after having examined the first half dozen hides from the pile.

"I don't read the brand, though," Waco commented, looking at an outline something like a letter "V" with two curved lines joining them together above it.

"I do," the blond giant said grimly. "That's the 'Beefhead,' boy. Which's how 'Front de Boeuf' comes out from French to English. It's my Uncle Winston's brand."

"I still think you've behaved in an improper fashion, regardless of *whose* brand it might be," Sangster claimed indignantly. "And we'll hear what Captain Fog has to say about your behaviour when he gets back this evening."

CHAPTER FIFTEEN

For the Benefit Of
the American People

Strolling alone through the darkness, having forgotten a hand-kerchief when leaving for the party funded by Harland Tod-hunter which had been delayed a day due to the construction hands having been too tired to feel like celebrating on their return for the display of rapid track laying, Dusty Fog was in a thoughtful mood not in accord with the belated function at Finnegan's Bar And General Store. Although he was aware that he still owed Raymond Sangster a debt of gratitude for having saved his life, he was thinking, as he approached the converted Pullman car in which he had his temporary quarters, that he would not be sorry when the gang boss promised by the railroad magnate arrived and he could consider he had fulfilled his obligation.

The ploy employed by the small Texan at the construction area had proved successful so far as the visiting members of the Railroad Commission was concerned, but the situation he had found on returning with them to the base camp had re-moved most of the pleasure from it and increased the dissatis-faction he felt towards the New Englander's attitude and general behaviour. It had been apparent that the events which occurred in his absence had brought the hostility between Sangster and his three *amigos* to a point where some action was necessary to avert trouble. Waco's temper in particular was clearly approaching its breaking point and Dusty believed he might not be long enough removed from his previous way of life to be able to keep holding it in check in the face of such continued provocation. The last thing the small Texan wanted was for the youngster to revert to the way he was heading when they had first met.

On the other hand, Dusty was willing to admit Todhunter had behaved in an honourable and satisfactory fashion when hearing of the means by which the work crews were being supplied with meat. Looking less than pleased at having to make the admission, Sangster had said he was at the hunters' camp delivering payment for the work they had carried out— the accountant having declined vehemently to perform the task because of their obnoxious behaviour on previous occasions —and was unaware of the means they employed to do it. Obviously resenting how his own shortcomings in the matter had been exposed, the young New Englander had not concealed his antagonism towards Mark Counter, the Ysabel Kid and, most especially, Waco, when complaining about what had happened. To his equally apparent annoyance, his employer had expressed complete agreement with the way the Texans had dealt with the situation.

Pointing out that stealing cattle was not the way to ensure good relations with ranchers, who could provide an early source of profit for the railroad by using it to ship their cattle into Mulrooney instead of driving herds there on the hoof, Todhunter had praised Mark, the Kid, and Waco for having brought the slow-elking to light before it was discovered by the owner of the cattle thus arousing his animosity. However, because of the feelings such behaviour would cause, he had suggested it would not be politic to bring the matter to public attention by handing the hunters over to the nearest law enforcement agency. Therefore, backed by Dusty, he had ordered the hunters to put as much distance as possible between themselves and the railroad in the shortest time. Then he had instructed Sangster to contact and compensate the owner at the current price given in Mulrooney for every animal taken.

Pointing out the meat supply would have to be kept up, the New Englander had sought to regain some of his loss of face by demanding rather than suggesting the work should be taken over by the three otherwise unoccupied Texans. He had clearly considered Dusty would back him on the issue when they declined to take part in what they regarded as the wholesale butchery of wild animals rather than the sport they had been contemplating before Waco had aroused their interest in the way meat was being supplied to the railroad. Nor had Sangster improved the situation by saying he felt they should do something to earn their living if they were to remain on railroad property. Dusty's immediate and angry offer to pay for their food and accommodation, backed by Mark—who had independent means beyond his wages from the OD Connected—was just as instantly rejected by Todhunter in a declaration that they were to be considered his guests.

In the face of such an outlook on the part of Sangster, even though he did not feel his own debt was discharged sufficiently to justify leaving himself, Dusty had been relieved to be given a reason to remove two of his companions from the presence of the New Englander. Having expressed satisfaction with what they had seen, showing a shrewdness which suggested he was better employed in the British diplomatic service than might have proved the case had he followed along standing family tradition by taking a commission in the Royal Navy,[1] Sir John Uglow Ramage had hinted he, Lord James Roxton and Jean Pierre Radisson would not be averse to doing some hunting on the way back to Mulrooney if they had somebody to act as guides. Guessing what lay behind the comment, Dusty had asked whether his *amigos* would be interested in taking on the chore. Considering the circumstances would be close to what they had envisaged and having developed a liking for the two English aristocrats in particular during their earlier acquaintance, the Kid and Waco had agreed. However, Mark had said he would set out to try and locate his uncle's ranch and explain about how the slow-elking of Beefhead cattle had been handled, hoping to ensure it did not produce a hostile response against the railroad. Such had been the

1. *Sir John Uglow Ramage was the youngest grandson of Admiral of the Fleet, the Eleventh Earl of Blazey, details of whose career in the Royal Navy prior to succeeding the title and reaching that high rank are recorded in the RAMAGE series of biographies by Dudley Pope.*

strength of ill feeling aroused by Sangster that all three had left that morning.

Although he missed his *amigos*' company, the small Texan had been looking forward to the celebration that evening. Nor had he been put off too greatly by Todhunter insisting that Sangster, who had not troubled to try and conceal his dislike of being compelled to mingle with the work force, attended. It was quickly made obvious to Dusty that he was held in even higher regard by the gandy dancers since the inspection and everything appeared set for a most pleasant party until the discovery that he did not have a handkerchief caused him to take what he anticipated to be a brief and uneventful departure.

A flicker of light showing through a window in the converted Pullman car diverted the small Texan from his thoughts. It was only brief and disappeared as the curtains were closed. Nevertheless, he found it disturbing. Although he knew a lantern was hanging alight in the passage between the cubicles and that all had similar illumination supplied for the occupants, the one to which his attention was drawn was Sangster's office and he remembered it had been in darkness when they set out for the party. Nor had anybody with the authority to be inside it left Finnegan's Bar.

Despite there having been no deliberate actions to interfere in any way with the construction of the railroad—except those by Richard Reiser and the Russians which Dusty did not learn of until much later—certain events in Mulrooney had led Dusty to consider something strange might be amiss. Therefore, he had not allowed himself to be lulled into a sense of false security. Rather he was aware that sufficient time had elapsed for the man who had hired killers to have replaced the men that Dusty had wiped out when they refused to surrender and accept arrest. Therefore, ever since his arrival at the base camp, he had remained on alert for anything out of the ordinary which could warn of a resumption of the attempts.

Without the need for conscious thought, the left side Colt 1860 Army Model revolver came swiftly into the small Texan's right hand. Then, feeling grateful that he had removed his spurs as being unnecessary for his work as gang boss, he began to make his way as quietly as he could to the entrance of the car. It was ajar and he eased it until wide enough for him to pass through. Still maintaining his silent approach, he arrived at the door of the office. Jerking it open, he went through fast and with the gun ready for instant use. On crossing the threshold, he discovered that he had *not* imagined there was somebody in the office cubicle who had no authority to be there.

"What the *hell*!" the interloper ejaculated in the accent of a well educated Easterner, straightening up and turning from where he was examining a map spread open on Sangster's desk.

However, the tone was not in accord with what Dusty had previously heard from the man. In his early twenties, tall and powerfully built, he had longish shaggy blond hair and a bushy beard which prevented his features, apart from his nose and blue eyes, from being seen. His attire was that of a gandy dancer and, as far as the small Texan's experienced gaze could detect, he was unarmed.

"What're you doing, Swede?" Dusty demanded, employing the sobriquet by which he knew the interloper.

"I ban come to see Mr. Sangster about something," the man replied, speaking with the somewhat lilting accent frequently employed by people of a Scandinavian origin—the tone to which the small Texan was accustomed.

"I *might* have believed that if your voice hadn't changed when I came in," Dusty said quietly, without relaxing his vigilance or lowering the Colt from its rock steady alignment. He knew the interloper to be very strong and capable of swift movement when necessary, so was taking no chances. "And knowing you'd seen him down to Finnegan's."

While speaking, the small Texan was remembering other things about the man he was confronting. Going by the name, "Olaf Olsen," his accent had always suggested a Scandinavian birth. Despite his comparative youth, he had proved himself so good at his duties and possessed of the ability to make others work under his guidance, that Dusty had made him one of the assistant gang bosses. However, although the small Texan had not attached any significance to the matter, he had always contrived to keep at a distance when Sangster paid a visit to the construction area. What was more, he had left the other gandy dancers when the members of the Railroad Commission were approaching yesterday and did not return until they were going away.

"All right, Captain Fog," the man said, giving a shrug and losing the accent. "I know what Ray Sangster did for you, but I don't think you class him as a *friend* and you certainly *aren't* his kind. So I'll tell you the truth. My name is Harland Todhunter, Junior—I see you've heard about me and I bet it wasn't from dad."

"Ray told me how come he got the chore of building the line instead of you," Dusty admitted.

"He didn't tell you all of it," the young man stated. "Somebody at the party spiked what should have been a reasonably harmless bowl of punch with some kind of alcohol and things got real wild, but we never found out who, or how the faculty got to know what was happening. I'd never got on with the Dean for various reasons, mainly because he'd a real mean hate for dad, so he jumped at the chance to kick me out before I had a chance to graduate. Dad got riled over the report of the incident he was sent and wouldn't listen to my side of it and —well, I left home. But I knew how much he'd got at stake in this railroad, and, when I heard he'd put Ray in charge, I decided I'd best come out to keep an eye on things."

"Ray didn't recognize you?"

"Not with my hair grown longer than I had it in college and this beard. Mom's maiden name was 'Olsen' and I've spent enough time with her side of the family to be able to put on a Norwegian accent well enough to get by. I made sure I didn't get too close to him and, anyway, he's not the kind to look over carefully at the men working under him. I could see things weren't going well and did what I could to help, but I've never been more relieved than when you showed up to take over as gang boss from Reiser."

"So why're you here?" Dusty demanded, returning the Colt to its holster. However, it was the sincerity underlying the story and not the compliment which led him to do so. "In *here*, I mean."

"I've been getting a feeling that we're not following the route picked out by the original survey. It was selected so as to cross unclaimed range, but we aren't sticking to it."

"You're *sure* of that?"

"Take a look," Harland Todhunter Junior offered, gesturing to the map and, on Dusty joining him, he ran his finger across it some distance to the east of the line indicating the route being taken. "Dad intended we should lay track this way, but here's where we're doing it. Although the man who has a ranch along where we're heading hasn't laid claim to the land, dad insisted we went by his boundary and not across it. But, the way we're going, that's what we'll do when we get over the Platte River and I don't reckon he'll be any too pleased when he finds out."

"I'd go along with you on *that*," Dusty admitted and felt as if he was being touched by a cold hand.

Except for four which had no mark of ownership, the hides at the meat hunters' camp had all carried the Beefhead brand. Their number suggested they had come from that ranch's range rather than being strays and they belonged to Mark Counter's uncle, Winston Front de Boeuf.

"What I can't understand is *why* Ray's changed the route," Junior declared.

"I reckon I can," Dusty said, suspecting the young man was aware of the reason and trying him out. "And, comes morning, you and me're going to find out if *we're* right."

"We're right about following this cattle trail being easier going than crossing open range," Harland Todhunter Junior commented, as he and Dusty Fog drew rein on a rim and looked down at the Platte River. "And, providing it's as strongly made as Reiser claimed, having a bridge there already will save the time needed to put one across.

"Why sure," the small Texan replied. "That's why we *both* reckoned the change of route was made."

Despite the assumption he had drawn, Dusty had elected to make no mention of the information given to him by "Swede Olsen." He had suspected that the railroad magnate would be disinclined to accept it on learning who had brought it to his attention and had not wished to cause trouble until he had put his theory to the test. Therefore, after replacing the map and making sure there was no trace of their visit to the office, he and Junior had gone to Finnegan's Bar to join the festivities without Todhunter Senior—who would probably have seen through the disguise—being given an opportunity to discover the latter was present.

That morning, the paint stallion and a mount for Junior having been brought to the construction area in the horse box which Dusty had had Tom Riordan—the Colonel being in use—add to the work train, they had set out to test the theory they shared. The small Texan had not been questioned about his intentions for the day by Todhunter Senior or Raymond Sangster. Nor had the other assistant gang bosses asked any questions when he told them to keep the construction going while he and "Swede Olsen" rode ahead to look at the bridge they would be using to cross the Platte River. It was such a basic precaution that doing so aroused no suspicions. There was, he learned as he and Junior were riding along, another reason for the acceptance of his selection of a companion. Shamus O'Sullivan, Louis "Frenchy" Rastignac and Fritz "Dutchy" Voigt were aware of the true state of affairs and, agreeing with the motive behind it, were willing to keep "Olsen's" true identity secret.

Having covered the mile or so from the construction area at a leisurely trot, the two young men had soon come into sight of the river. As was often the case when a continuous supply of water was available to stimulate the growth of trees and bushes, unlike on the rolling open country they had been traversing, there was a fairly wide coating of woodland on each bank. However, the trail originally made by great numbers of buffalo was sufficiently wide to remove any need for it to be enlarged before the railroad track could pass through.

"Give Reiser his due," Junior commented on arriving at the southern bank and looking at the very sturdy wooden structure over the swiftly flowing current. "He might have been a lousy liber-rad queer, but he was right about this bridge. It'll take plenty of weight. In fact, with some strengthening, there won't be any need to replace it for regular use. He did a good job of work finding it."

"That he did," Dusty admitted, albeit his tone indicated he had reservations on the point.

"Except?" Junior hinted, suspecting that once again the *big* Texan and he were thinking along similar lines.

Although he did not reply immediately, Dusty's doubts were not over whether the bridge was suitable to take the railroad over the river. Instead, he was reading the information painted in large red letters on a white wooden board which was attached to the right side end post of the sturdy guard rail.

> "THIS BRIDGE WAS CONSTRUCTED BY
> THE UNITED STATES ARMY'S
> CORPS OF ENGINEERS
> IN 1868 FOR THE BENEFIT OF
> THE AMERICAN PEOPLE"

"Man'd say they did a right good job of work 'for the benefit of the people,'" Dusty remarked dryly, looking at his companion after a few seconds. "Only that sign's a whole heap more recent than '68, unless somebody's been around not too long back to keep the paint freshened."

"That's what I thought," Junior replied. "Does the Army's Corps of Engineers do much of this sort of thing?"

"Not that I've heard tell of," the small Texan replied. "They do build bridges, but even though having one here would help ranchers north of the Platte to get their trail herds down to the railroad in Kansas easier than swimming over, I wouldn't've expected them to be sent to put one out here. Nebraska Territory doesn't have the kind of money to fund it and likely it wouldn't be thought important enough to get votes for the politicians in Washington, D.C., to have the Federal Government hand over the cash. Top of which, what I know about the Army, this being a place where the bridge isn't likely to get seen and talked about by anybody important enough to get credit and promotion for whoever planned it, the top brass of the Corps of Engineers wouldn't do it of their own accord."

"*Somebody* must have had it built," Junior commented, having been thinking along much the same lines. "And dad wasn't behind it, or the track would have been routed this way instead of where he chose."

"Like you say, *amigo*," Dusty drawled. "*Somebody* must've had it built. Let's go over and see happen we can find out who that 'somebody' was. Because, should they have paid for it out of their own pockets—which I reckon's likely—they're not going to take kind' to having the railroad just come along and take it over. I likely shouldn't be saying this to *you*, but railroads have got kind of a bad name for riding rough-shod over other folks' property elsewhere."

"You don't have to tell *me* what kind of reputation the railroads have got elsewhere," Junior declared. "That's why dad was so insistent on not going over land anybody else had already claimed and was using, even if they hadn't taken legal title to it." Then anger came to his face and he went on, "God damn it. By coming this way because he figured it would be easier, Ray Sangster's going to do the one thing dad wanted to avoid!"

"Then we'd best go see happen we can find out who had it built and set things to rights," Dusty declared and started his horse moving.

However, as the two young men were riding across the bridge, they discovered they were not alone in the area.

"Keep coming slow and easy!" a masculine voice with a Texan's accent called from among the trees on the northern bank. "And, happen you know what's good for you, you'll keep your hands well away from your guns."

CHAPTER SIXTEEN

My Daddy Built That Bridge

"Get down," the voice commanded, still without the speaker revealing himself, as Dusty Fog and Harland Todhunter Junior reached the northern end of the bridge. "And, afore you get any smart notions, there're enough guns covering you from *both* sides of the trail to stop 'em working."

Wondering who and what they might be up against, the small Texan swung his right foot forward over the low horn of the double girthed saddle so he could drop from the big paint stallion with both hands in view, yet be more ready for immediate action than would have been possible by dismounting in the conventional manner. The voice sounded cautious rather than harsh and deliberately pitched to be menacing, but he was disinclined to take any chances until he had formed a better estimation of the situation. Glancing sideways, he was pleased to see his companion was doing as commanded in a fashion which indicated a lack of hostile intentions.

Satisfied Junior was avoiding any action which might provoke a hostile response, Dusty turned his gaze to the figures emerging from their places of concealment amongst the bushes and trees. All wore range clothing, with styles varying between Texas and the northern cattle country. While they held rifles and had revolvers, the rigs upon which the latter were carried did not have the appearance of being designed with really fast withdrawal as the prime consideration. Except for one of them, they struck him as the kind of hard working and honest cowhands with whom he spent much of his life.

Dressed after the same fashion as the others and holding a Winchester Model of 1866 carbine with an air of being proficient in its use, the exception was a girl in her early twenties. Tall and shapely, as far as her attire allowed her figure to be seen, she had a tanned beautiful face with strength of will and determination in its lines. What little hair showed from beneath her low crowned and wide brimmed tan Stetson of Texas' style was golden blonde.

"What brings you hereabouts?" the exception asked, also in the manner of a Texan.

"We work for the railroad spur-line that's being built this way," Dusty replied.

"I didn't take your *amigo* for a *cowhand*," the girl declared in the tone of one long used to speaking with men on their own level. "You wouldn't be meat-hunting for the railroad now would you?" Although she paused briefly, she went on in a hostile manner before either the small Texan or Junior could speak, "'Cause happen you are and have been doing it over this side of the Platte, you might like to tell us how come you *mistook* a bunch of our Beefhead steers on their home range for wild critters."

"More'n *once*, happen all the sign reads right," supplemented the next to oldest of the cowhands, a deeply bronzed and leathery faced man with an air of command about him and his voice proved it was he who had done the speaking up to that point.

"You'll be Winston Front de Boeuf's daughter, I'd say," Dusty drawled, watching the group moving forward slowly and with caution.

"We all know who I am," the girl asserted. "So who're *you*?"

"Dusty Fog," the small Texan replied.

"*Dusty Fog*," the girl repeated in a tone of disbelief which was clearly shared by her companions. "And this'll be cousin Mar—*Mark Counter*, or is he the Ysabel Kid?"

"Neither, ma'am," the young Easterner denied and removed his derby hat to perform a graceful bow. "Harland Todhunter Junior, at your service."

"*You* are Dusty Fog?" the girl challenged, without so much as glancing at, much less acknowledging Junior's words and gesture.

"I have been for a fair spell now," the small Texan replied and thought of a way he might prove his *bona-fides*. "And, although I don't know what your folks called you when you was baptized, I'll bet you *wasn't* named for your Aunt Jessica Front de Boeuf, going by what Mark's told me about her and your Cousin Trudeau."

"That's an OD Connected brand on the paint, Tony," one of the younger cowhands commented while the girl was digesting the substance of the comment. "But I've allus heard tell Dusty Fog was real *big*—!"

"I'm big enough," the small Texan drawled, having long since stopped being concerned or resentful when such remarks were made. "My feet touch the ground when I'm standing up."

"That's *allus* a way of deciding," the original spokesman admitted, studying Dusty with experienced eyes which saw beyond mere physical appearances. A man would need to be very well versed in handling horses to sit that big paint stallion instead of winding up on the ground and, likely, picking its iron shod hooves out of his teeth. What was more, the twin white handled Colt 1860 Army Model revolvers and the rig he was wearing did not look to be the affectation of one trying to look tough. All in all, there was an air about him suggesting there was vastly more to him than met the eye. "Where-at's Mark and the Kid, Cap'n Fog?"

"Mark's headed up this way trying to find your spread so's he can visit for a spell, Miss Front de Boeuf," Dusty explained, seeing the other cowhands were willing to accept his identity in view of the tall man's response. "I reckon he'd be going along this trail hoping it'd take him there."

"It will," confirmed Antonia Front de Boeuf, although she was generally known as "Tony," also lowering her rifle. She too sensed the true potential of the *big* Texan. Furthermore, although they had not met since they were children, she felt sure Mark Counter would only tell a man he trusted implicitly the unsavoury truth about their Aunt Jessica and Cousin Trudeau and, going by all she had heard since the end of the War Between The States, Dusty Fog would come into that exclusive category. "We came across the range from where we found a whole bunch of Beefhead cattle'd been shot and butchered, so we must've missed him."

"It was made slow-elk by the hunters the railroad hired," Dusty confessed. "But we caught them at it and Harl' here's pappy, who's having it built, will pay you full market price at Mulrooney for all that's been brought in."

"We didn't know they were slow-elking, Miss Front de Boeuf, but you can rest assured they *won't* be doing any more of it," Junior asserted. "And we'll *buy* the rest we'll need to feed the crew at the same price."

"*Sounds* reasonable enough," Tony admitted. However, her thoughts on how profitable the arrangement would prove were diverted by another consideration of more immediate importance. "We didn't know the railroad was coming *this* way. Fact being, we got told it'd go west of here and clear of our range."

"Seems the man in charge of building it figured it'd be easier going along this cattle trail," Dusty explained. "Especially when he heard about the bridge here's the Army's Corps of Engineers put across the river—!"

"*Who* put it across?" Tony demanded indignantly.

"That's what the sign on the other side says," Junior explained.

"*Sign?*" the girl queried. "I've been over both ways a helluva heap of times and never seen no god-damned *sign!*"

"There's one on the post at the other end," Junior elaborated, noticing for the first time that the same did not apply where they were standing.

"Then I don't know who the hell put it there!" the girl snapped. "What's more, I don't give a damn what any sign says. My daddy built this bridge!"

"I thought that sign looked kind of new," Dusty drawled, guessing what had happened and wondering whether the board had been placed there at Sangster's instigation or if it was Richard Reiser's idea to prevent the true state of affairs from being suspected when the construction of the track reached the river.

Before any more could be said, the oldest of the cowhands provided a distraction. Agony was twisting at his sweat-soaked face and, dropping his Henry rifle, he clutched at his stomach then collapsed.

"What's wrong, Ben?" the girl gasped and an aura of concern came to her attractive expressive features.

"He's been saying his stomach hurt all morning," one of the younger cowhands answered when the old man did not reply. "We wanted him to go back to the spread, but you know what he's like."

"I *know*. Tony agreed, but there was gentleness in the way she knelt by and looked at the obviously suffering old man. "Get over to Templeton and fetch the doctor to the spread one of you!"

"There's a doctor closer than that," Junior pointed out, remembering what he had seen on the map he had studied the previous evening and thinking how fortuitous it was that the railroad's well liked medical practitioner had elected to spend the day at the construction area. "I'd say it would be quicker to have him come here."

"I'll go fetch him," Dusty offered. "It's time this old paint of mine had him a good run. I'll have to take your horse for him, Harl."

"That livery stable plug'll slow you down," Tony put in, before Junior could speak. "Take me *grulla* and the best two of the boys' horses, Cap'n Fog. Ben's a worthless ole cuss, but I'd sooner he got well even if he's only suffering from eating too much."

"We'll do *everything* we can to make sure he does," the small Texan promised, knowing the true sentiments behind words which had tried to sound unemotional and guessing the offer of the *grulla* would not have been made in less dire circumstances. "Count on us for that."

"It sounds like he's suffering from appendicitis," Doctor Brian Farnsworth estimated, having listened to what Dusty Fog had to say on returning hurriedly to the construction area. "And if it is, I can't handle it here or even at the base camp."

"Where's the nearest place you could?" the small Texan wanted to know.

Having used all the skill at riding acquired over a lifetime spent in the saddle, including the years during and since the War Between The States when he had frequently needed to travel fast in order to avoid capture or death at the hands of enemies, the small Texan had made good time back to the construction area. Although certain he could count on the medical practitioner for every possible assistance, he was pleased to see Harland Todhunter Senior had come with Raymond Sangster—presumably by hand-car—from the base camp. Recollecting what he had been told by Marvin Eldridge "Doc" Leroy of the Wedge trail crew,[1] he was aware of how serious appendicitis could be and, despite having every confidence in Farnsworth's ability, had believed it could not be dealt with at the bridge should that be what ailed the old cowhand. He was prepared to take whatever steps might be necessary to help the doctor, but realized the railroad magnate could give even more assistance should the need arise.

"Doctor Cosgrove has everything we'd need at Mulrooney," Farnsworth replied. "Including a surgery equipped for the operation."

"Then, should you need," Todhunter said, without even glancing at Dusty, having listened to the conversation. "We'll get him there."

"How?" Sangster inquired and, although he did not say, "Why should we?" it was implied in his tone.

1. *Information about the career of Marvin Eldridge "Doc" Leroy can be found in: Part Five, "The Hired Butcher,"* THE HARD RIDERS; *Part Three, "The Invisible Winchester,"* OLE DEVIL'S HANDS AND FEET; *Part Five, "A Case of Infectious Plumbeus Veneficium,"* THE FLOATING OUTFIT; *Part Three, "Monday Is A Quiet Day,"* THE SMALL TEXAN; *Part Two, "Jordan's Try,"* THE TOWN TAMERS; RETURN TO BACKSIGHT; *Part Six, "Keep Good Temper Alive"* J.T.'S HUNDREDTH *and the Waco series. Although he had not achieved his ambition to become a qualified doctor at the period of this narrative, how he did so is described in:* DOC LEROY, M.D.

1a. *The Wedge acted as a contract rail crew for groups of ranchers who had too few cattle to consider making up and delivering a herd individually as a viable prospect. They make "guest" appearances in:* QUIET TOWN; TRIGGER FAST; *Part One, "To Separate Innocence From Guilt,"* MORE J.T.'S LADIES *and* GUN WIZARD. *They also "star" in their own right in:* BUFFALO ARE COMING!

"By the work train," the railroad magnate replied. "Get *everything* that isn't absolutely necessary cleared off it."

"But there might not be any need," the young New Englander protested.

"There might not," Todhunter agreed. "But, happen there is, I don't want any damned delay if we find out the feller's got appendicitis when he's brought here." Then swinging his gaze from Sangster, he continued, "Go and do what needs doing, Doc!"

"Do you know something, Dusty?" Farnsworth asked, while he and the small Texan were riding northwards along the trail. "That's the *first* time Mr. Todhunter's called me 'Doc.'"

"He's a man I can like," Dusty replied. "I know helping that old cowhand'll put him in good with the Front de Boeufs right when he needs *that* bad—!"

"You mean because of the slow-elking?" the doctor guessed, before the comment could be completed.

"And that," the small Texan said cryptically, but decided against mentioning the unauthorized change of route. "Only I'd bet everything I've got that he'd have done the same anyways and, which being, that's my kind of *man*."

"I agree," the doctor declared without hesitation, having failed to draw any conclusions from the first part of the answer. "But I wish he hadn't split up with the young Harland. That's how Ray Sangster came to be put in charge."

"Could be they'll make it up again," Dusty suggested, but the need to concentrate on getting the best possible speed out of the horses prevented him from being asked to explain his second cryptic—yet hopeful in this case—remark.

"Get *everything* unloaded off the flat cars, Ray!" Todhunter commanded, being unaware of the remarks passing between Dusty and Farnsworth as they rode away and giving his attention to what might lie ahead.

"*Everything?*" Sangster repeated, frowning with a lack of comprehension.

"*Everything,*" the railroad magnate confirmed. "Rails, sleepers, tools, the whole god-damned lot. I want those cars emptied so's what they're carrying can be used after the train's gone back with the feller who's sick."

"But there might not be any *need*—!"

"Then we'll have 'em loaded again."

"But the delay—!"

"There's been so much *delay* already that the bit extra won't make any difference," Todhunter said, eyeing Sangster coldly, and he raised his voice to a bellow. "Tom Riordan! Mose Jones!" When the engineer and his black fireman arrived on the run, he went on in an amiable tone, "Could be you'll have to take a sick man to Mulrooney as quick as it can be done, Tom, Mose."

"Then you couldn't get it done no quicker any other way, boss," Riordan declared. "Could he, Mose?"

"Not without sprouting wings and flying," the fireman seconded.

"Something told me you'd say *that*," the railroad magnate asserted with a grin. Then he became serious. "Should it happen, what'll you need to get the best speed?"

"Plenty of wood for the boiler, enough water to keep a good head of steam and the best journal oil to stop a hot box, which we've already got," Riordan replied. "There's only one thing I'd ask for."

"It's yours if it can be had," Todhunter stated.

"There won't be no trouble afore we've got the Colonel facing south at Fogville, which's what we've started to call the base camp," the engineer declared with confidence. "But we'll only take along the caboose, happen it's all right with you."

"You're doing the driving, Tom," the railroad magnate authorized.

"Right then," Riordan said, nodding approval. "With the speed we'll be going, I want every switch 'tween there and Mulrooney spiked shut tight to cut any chance of us jumping the track."

"You've got *it*!" Todhunter promised. "Ray, have the telegraph crew here send back for things to be got ready to do it as soon as I give the word, and tell 'em if there's any mistake, the man who makes it will *never* work on another railroad as long as he lives."

"You're taking all this much trouble just for a *cowhand*?"

Sangster inquired sourly, instead of going immediately to carry out the instruction.

"I'm doing it for a sick man," Todhunter corrected coldly. "And, if you can't understand *that*, you're no man to be running the building of *my* railroad."

CHAPTER SEVENTEEN

It Was *Him* Who Hired Us

"Here comes the Colonel!" Harland Todhunter Junior said.

"I wish we'd heard *something*!" Antonia Front de Boeuf replied, also looking to where the engine—still with only the caboose attached—was approaching at a more leisurely pace than when it had departed shortly before noon.

"They do say no news is *good* news, Tony," Dusty Fog drawled in a soothing fashion. Then he grinned disarmingly as the girl swung towards him with annoyance on her beautiful face. "Which, afore you tell me, isn't a whole heap of comfort when you're real worried about somebody."

"*Worried*?" Tony yelped, seeking relief from her anxiety by a pretence at indifference. "Who'd be *worried* about what happens to a worn out, ornery old cuss like Ben Cull?"

"Well, if you *aren't*," Junior said with a sympathetic grin, watching the play of emotion which gave the lie to the outburst. "You'll do until somebody who is *worried* comes along."

Arriving at the bridge, Doctor Brian Farnsworth had only needed a quick examination to conclude the old cowhand had collapsed with an acute attack of appendicitis and declare only an operation would save him. The medical practitioner had made no attempt to minimize the risks involved, not the least being transporting him to where it could be carried out, but he had also stressed it was the only way to save his life.

The youngest of the cowhands, asking why it was necessary to take Ben to Mulrooney instead of removing the appendix on the spot, said he had heard Doc Leroy had done the same operation after rendering the sufferer unconscious

149

with a blow from an empty whiskey bottle and using a borrowed bowie knife to operate. Before the doctor could reply, Dusty, saying he hated to spoil the story for his *amigo* from the Wedge, had explained it had become considerably embellished in the telling. While Doc had kept a man from dying of acute appendicitis during a trail drive, working far from the nearest town, he had employed the whiskey and not the bottle in lieu of a conventional anaesthetic and the set of surgeon's instruments he carried in his father's medical bag with the rest of his "thirty years" gatherings.

With the point settled, Tony had inquired whether the operation would prove successful. Admitting frankly he could not guarantee the result, taking into account the patient's age and the need to go so far before it could be performed, Farnsworth reiterated the belief that nothing else would keep him alive. Without taking time to consult with even the second oldest of the cowhands—who was introduced as Mike Hazeltine, *segundo* of the Beefhead ranch—the girl had reached what was obviously a very difficult decision and had given her consent. What was more, while Dusty was collecting the doctor from the construction area, she had had an Indian-style *travois* made from branches and shirts donated by Junior and the younger men of her party.

While the Easterner had shown he would like to remain in Tony's company, he had accepted that neither Dusty's big paint stallion nor any of the cow ponies used by the Beefhead hands would be suitable for pulling the *travois* and he had surrendered his horse without hesitation. Placing the old man on it and making him secure, the girl had said she and Hazeltine would accompany him at least as far as the base camp and for the rest to take Harl—as they were now calling him—back to the ranch where her father would want to express gratitude. Pointing out that such a visit would allow the matter of the slow-elking to be concluded in a way satisfactory to both sides, and believing this would strengthen his chances of affecting a reconciliation between Todhunter Senior and Junior, the small Texan had given his support to the suggestion.

The first part of the journey had been accomplished with-

out difficulty or without adding to Cull's suffering more than
was absolutely necessary, such was the excellence of the way
the *travois* had been constructed. By the time they reached the
construction area, goaded by the orders and example set by
Todhunter Senior, the gandy dancers had everything ready for
the next stage. The flat cars had been unloaded and all that
was needed had been to make the patient as comfortable as
possible in the caboose. However, although the magnate
stated his intention of going along, Farnsworth had prevailed
upon the girl and her *segundo* to stay behind. In the circumstances, realizing it might prove a lengthy process, Dusty refrained from mentioning the presence and behavior of Junior
to his father. After the train left, building up a far higher speed
than the small Texan had previously seen, Tony and Hazeltine
spent the intervening time watching the construction work and
trying to relax by making casual conversation with Dusty and
the assistant gang bosses. No word had come from
Mulrooney. However, as the sun was going down, they had
been told the Colonel was returning and they had gone to meet
it.

Under less trying conditions, having learned how Tom
Riordan would only carry people he considered worthy of the
privilege in the cab, Dusty might have been at least puzzled at
seeing a man wearing range clothes standing behind him and
the fireman. Nor, although it brought a number of the gandy
dancers hurrying over from their accommodation, did the
small Texan attach any importance—other than thinking it
was the engineer's way of announcing the operation had
proved successful—to the repeated whooping call of the
Colonel's whistle as it was approaching. His first inkling that
all was far from well came as the engine was brought to a halt
in front of him and he saw the Colt 1860 Army Model revolver which the man was holding.

However, the realization that something was badly wrong
came an instant too late!

"Don't *nobody* try *nothing*!" bawled a voice with an Illinois accent, as half a dozen men dressed in various Western
styles and holding guns began to leap from the doors at each
end of the caboose. "We've got Harland Todhunter hawg-tied

to a chair in here with a sawed-off ten gauge in his favourite gut and he'll get both barrels should there be *any* fuss at all."

"Don't *anybody* make a move!" Dusty instructed in a carrying voice, seeing Shamus O'Sullivan, Louis "Frenchy" Rastignac, Fritz "Dutchy" Voigt and the Molloy brothers in the forefront of the crowd and knowing none of them, or the others, were armed.

"That's *real* smart, short stu—!" the speaker praised, proving to be wearing the attire of a successful professional gambler and holding an Army Colt in his right hand, as he came from the front end of the caboose, followed by Michael Meacher.

"That's *Dusty Fog*, Mr. Short," the young man put in urgently.

"*Him*?" David Short snorted.

"I know he don't *look* it," Meacher admitted, once again becoming aware of the small Texan's true height on seeing him in less demanding circumstances and with a girl by his side to serve as a comparison. "But he's Dusty Fog for sure."

"Yeah," Short said quietly, having studied the small Texan more closely and reaching accurate conclusions regarding his potential. "I reckon he is at that."

"There's no pay roll due for a couple weeks at most," Dusty said, allowing his hands to dangle by his sides well clear of his weapons. Although he felt sure such was not the reason for the visit, he continued as if believing it to be the case, "So, should this be a hold up, you've come a fair way for poor pickings."

"It's no *hold up*," Short corrected. "And I don't for a moment reckon you think it is, Cap'n Fog. I've come to settle accounts for my nephew's you downed when him and this knob-head tried to gun you down."

"They didn't give me a whole heap of choice in the matter," Dusty pointed out, having suspected the motive and watching the armed men spreading along the side of the track in front of the train so as to be able to keep the growing crowd covered.

"So the knob-head said," Short conceded. "Trouble being

I've spread word's *nobody* was to do *anything* to him on account of him being something special to me."

"*He* was *special* to you?" the small Texan asked, being genuinely puzzled at an outlaw with a sizeable price on his head being willing to chance seeking revenge for the killing of a man like Ronald "Rocky" Todd.

"I know it don't sound *likely*," Short admitted frankly, suffering from no illusions where his nephew was concerned. "Trouble being, his momma's got a helluva a lot of my money stashed away back to home and, knowing her, she'd use me not getting evens for him as an excuse to hang on to it should I let things pass. So I've just natural' got to do *something* about you making wolf bait of him."

"*You*," Dusty queried, his manner derisive and challenging. "Or you *and* all these fellers you've brought along for backing?"

An interruption came before the outlaw leader could reply.

"Mr. Short, sir!" Meacher put in urgently, pointing to a man who was coming to the forefront of the crowd. "It was *him* who hired us, and then warned Cap'n Fog when we was coming out to gun him down without him expecting it."

Resenting the rebuke he had received from Todhunter Senior, Raymond Sangster had spent the afternoon sulking in his quarters. However, on hearing the train returning, curiosity had compelled him to put in an appearance. Seeing the finger pointed at him and hearing the statement by the survivor of the abortive attempt to kill Dusty Fog, he realized the decision had put him in a very dangerous position.

Pampered by his middle class-middle management parents, and filled with a sense of his mental superiority almost from birth, Raymond Sangster had later found this quality more imaginary than real. When setting out for college he had been confident he would easily make his mark on life. But while he had been completing an education paid for by his doting father, to fit him for a senior position in engineering projects, he had become aware that book-learning would not be enough to set him above others in that line of endeavour. However, unlike many of his kind when making a similar discovery, he had not adopted "liberal" persuasions and proclaimed a complete disinterest in the financial benefits of success as an easy way of avoiding failure in his chosen field. Instead, satisfied that he was well equipped in theory, he had sought for a means of utilizing his talents lucratively.

Getting to know the Todhunters had offered a way for the New Englander. He was aware of the hostility between the father and the Dean of the college and saw how it might be turned to his advantage if the latter was given cause to gloat because of the son's failure to graduate. Unfortunately, Harland Junior, despite giving the impression of being relaxed and more interested in taking part in various sporting activities— attaining considerable proficiency in all of them, whereas Sangster could not succeed at any—and having fun rather than study, he was such a good student that no reason was likely to occur for him to fail to graduate. However, an opportunity was presented by the celebration following the successful outcome of a Boston game against the team's strongest rivals, the University of Notre Dame. The Dean had expressed disapproval in very strong terms of the rowdy and high spirited behaviour which accompanied previous successes and had given dire warnings of the consequences if these should be continued.

Going to the party, Sangster had "spiked" what should have been comparatively harmless punch with pure alcohol obtained from the medical laboratory. Junior had been less culpable than the others, in fact he was trying to quieten them down when the police arrived in response to complaints about the noise from the neighbours, but the Dean had made the most of the chance by dismissing him, even though his final examination papers for graduation were awaiting adjudication. Having already ingratiated himself with Todhunter Senior, the New Englander had ensured the breach caused by the news would widen while pretending to try and seal it. Having ordered his son to leave home, the railroad magnate had offered Sangster the post of supervisor for the spur-line going north from Kansas which he was financing.

Again like many others of his kind, regardless of his parent's high opinion of his ability to get things done—with which he whole-heartedly concurred—the New Englander had found reality a vastly different proposition to his fantasies. The mental superiority which he had believed he possessed and which he expected would bring success had failed to produce the desired results. In fact, it had soon become apparent to him that he had neither the personality nor the capability to make the men over whom he was in charge work as well as was required to keep to the schedule of construction he promised. Coming into contact with a man who had all the qualities he lacked and realizing how this might be turned to his advantage, he had concocted a plot to bring it to fruition.

Knowing of the Southern code of honour to which he felt sure Dusty Fog adhered, Sangster had used this as the basis of his scheme. Hearing about the reputation of Honesty John's Tavern in Brownton, he had believed he could find the assistance he required there. Realizing he must not allow his true identity to be detected, he had made use of the skill in disguise and acting acquired as a member of the college's dramatic society to avoid being recognized. Watching the three would-be hired killers—being unaware that Ronald "Rocky" Todd's special relationship with David Short made using him inadvisable—he had concluded they were exactly what he required, and his subsequent negotiations had confirmed the supposition. He was satisfied that, even if they had failed to notice the clue he gave that he was a member of the Little family engaged on a quest for revenge against the small Texan, they had no idea who he really was or what he actually looked like.

What the New Englander had not known was that Michael Meacher had been in the vicinity of the rendezvous at Mulrooney during which he had outlined to Todd the methods to be employed for the ambush and, although failing to follow him to the Railroad House Hotel, Meacher saw him without his disguise. Confident he would not be recognized with the appearance he intended to adopt, and wanting to know if the truth might be suspected, after having "warned" the small Texan, he had sought to further ingratiate himself by offering to help procure information from the survivor of the trio. He was unaware that, once again, he had underestimated the shrewdness of Meacher, who had pierced his disguise at the jail, but could not decide the best way to utilize the knowledge. Wishing to emphasize the extent of his problems, also deriving satisfaction from the thought that he had proved his intellect superior over the very competent trio of Texans who had shown him none of the respect he felt should be his due and who, he realized, only accepted him because he had "saved" Dusty Fog from the ambush, the New Englander had resumed the disguise of "Will Little" and left the money at the Driven Spike Saloon which led to the confrontation between Dusty Fog and the gandy dancers.

Unfortunately for Sangster, although he had been successful in creating a debt of honour which the small Texan was obliged to repay, doing so had merely served to show his own inadequacies. He had come to hate Dusty for the respect and willingness to work hard displayed by the men and which had never been given to him. Until Meacher had spoken, hearing what passed between the small Texan and the leader of the invaders, he had believed he would have no further cause for annoyance on that score. Nor, despite being identified, did he consider he had any great reason for concern. He was confident that he would be able to refute the accusation and, because of its source, there would be no difficulty in having his version accepted.

Even as Sangster was reaching this conclusion, the situation changed rapidly!

Hearing the accusation made by Michael Meacher and being aware of their leader's feelings on the subject, every one of the outlaws started to look at the man he had indicated!

Doing so proved to be an error in tactics!

If they had given the matter consideration, none of the gang would have expected any trouble from the gandy dancers. They did not know of the high regard in which Dusty Fog was held by the men they were covering and they believed that, particularly when faced with the threat of weapons, they would be willing to leave him to his fate. In that, they made a very serious mistake. Even though the gandy dancers had also failed to respond to the alarm warning when hearing the whistle blasts given by Tom Riordan (who had given the pretence of this being his usual habit when ap-

proaching the base camp) they were alert for any possibility of
turning the tables on the outlaws.

Watching and waiting for an opportunity in the cab of the
engine, Riordan was the first to make the most of the one
being presented. What was more, the means he employed not
only proved most effective, but produced a very good diver-
sion. The moment that the outlaw keeping guard on them
looked away, catching Moses Jones' eyes and nodding, he
reached for and pushed down a lever. Instantly, there was a
hissing roar and a cloud of scalding hot steam was vented
through a pipe on the side of the boiler to engulf the member
of the gang standing just in front of it. Letting out a hideous
screech, he flung aside his revolver and staggered away with
his hands knocking off his hat to claw desperately at his head.

A startled exclamation burst from the outlaw in the cab and
he started to swing his gaze forward from glancing at
Meacher. Before he could find out what had caused the com-
motion and take action, he felt his shoulders seized by two big
and powerful hands. Swung around by the black fireman, with
no greater apparent difficulty than if he had been a babe in
arms, he found himself being propelled backwards. Although
his Colt went off, its bullet flew harmlessly into the front of
the control panel. Then he was pushed through the entrance on
the side furthest away from the disturbance, and crashed down
supine on the hard packed ground to lose all further interest in
what was happening.

The sounds of the screams reached into the caboose. Despite what his leader had said, the outlaw inside was not keeping the sawed-off shotgun pointing at the target described.
Instead, being cautious by nature, he had it positioned so he
could turn the twin barrels towards either Todhunter or the
conductor as the occasion demanded. Alarmed by what he
heard, his vigilance relaxed and this was acted upon with
commendable—albeit not from his point of view—rapidity
by both of his prisoners.

Thrusting himself from the chair upon which he had been
ordered to sit, the railroad magnate launched a tackle which
his son would have admired if performed in a Boston game.
Moving at the same moment, the conductor grabbed for the

Army Colt concealed under a rag on the shelf beneath his desk for use in such a situation. Before he could regain control of the situation, the outlaw was rammed in the chest by a bulky and still firmly fleshed body moving at considerable speed. Not only did the impact cause the weapon to discharge one of its nine buckshot loads into the opposite side with the recoil ripping in from his loosened grip, but he was also slammed against the wall of the caboose and had all the air driven from his lungs. The fist which crashed against his jaw to ensure he was rendered *hors de combat* was as unnecessary as the revolver which was directed his way by the conductor.

No more able than his men to resist looking at Sangster, Short presented Dusty with a chance. The instant the gang leader's weapon wavered from alignment, the small Texan responded with the rapidity which had saved his life on many occasions. Thrusting himself sideways a long pace, so as to gain the split second it would take for the weapon to be redirected his way, his hands were crossing while he was starting to move his feet. Out came the bone handled Army Colts, turning forward and roaring in unison. Realizing the mistake he was making, Short tried to correct it. He was too late. Before he could return his revolver to its previous point of aim, two .44 calibre bullets ripped into his chest and pitched him against the side of the engine.

Alarmed by the unanticipated turn of events, Raymond Sangster grabbed for the Remington Double Derringer he had carried in the right side pocket of his jacket—with the exception of the night he had "saved" Dusty, when he had no desire to take the chance of letting it be discovered he was armed—since coming West. He was not allowed to bring it out, much less put it to the use he intended. What was more, he was prevented from doing so by the man upon whom it was to be used.

Although Meacher had hoped to buy leniency by exposing the New Englander, or to blackmail him when set free instead of being sent to trial, the arrival of Short's men had prevented the latter. Wishing to avoid being held responsible for the death of Todd, he had told the outlaws that he knew who had paid for the abortive ambush and who, for some inexplicable reason, had warned the intended victim before it could succeed. Then he had offered to carry out the identification if given a chance.

When it was discovered that Sangster was with Dusty Fog at the railhead, Short had taken advantage of the train returning to get there more quickly than would be possible on horseback. He had also assumed, correctly, that arriving in such a manner would arouse less suspicion than riding up at the head of his gang. Having taken his revenge, he intended to force the engineer to take them back to Mulrooney, cutting the telegraph wire in more than one place along the track to prevent news of what had happened reaching the town until he was well on his way from it.

Brought along to point out the New Englander Meacher, although not being considered a member of the gang, had been allowed to retain his armament and had been ordered to help keep the gandy dancers under control by covering them with one of his revolvers. Seeing what Sangster was doing, he acted out of a mixture of self preservation and a desire to avenge the death of his two companions. Raising the Colt to eye level, he sighted and fired. Chance rather than accuracy guided the bullet into the New Englander's body, and, twirling around with the Remington flying from his hand, he sprawled down in a torrent of pain.

One of the remaining outlaws reacted more swiftly than his companions. Spluttering a profanity, he began to turn the rifle he was holding towards Dusty. Before he could complete the motion, giving vent to bellows of rage, the gandy dancers surged forward. Moving faster than the rest, Bob Molloy brought the man's attention and weapon in his direction. Alarmed by the expression of fury shown by the approaching Irishman, he panicked and snatched at the trigger before making sure of his aim. Although the bullet tore a furrow across Bob's ribs, fortunately continuing its flight without hitting any of the other gandy dancers, the wound was not sufficiently serious to deter him from his purpose. Hurtling through the air for the last few feet, he wrenched the rifle from its owner's grasp. Swinging it around with the precision a soldier trained in all aspects of bayonet fighting would have been hard pressed to better, he slammed the metal shod butt against the side of the man's head and brought a finish to any further danger from that source.

Nor did the rest of the gang fare any better. Seeing the way the gandy dancers were coming at them, prudence dictated their response. Instead of there being any attempt to use weapons in self defense, they were thrown aside unfired. While this did not save the outlaws from some rough handling, it was less severe than would have been the case if they had started shooting. In a few seconds, not one of them was still standing and the threat to Dusty Fog's life no longer existed.

"I got the son-of-a-bitch for you, Cap'n Fog!" Meacher said, having thrown aside his Colt and avoiding being included in the attack upon the outlaws. "It was him's hired us to gun you down. Then he went and yelled a warning to you, but I'm damned if I can figure out *why*!"

"I can," the small Texan said quietly, realizing what must have happened and thinking of the comment Todd had started to make just before he was killed. It had not been a statement of blame for what had occurred as a result of the warning, but because some trick of the light had enabled him to identify Sangster as "Will Little." Dusty turned his gaze downwards and the last words heard by the New Englander were, "The god-damned stupid fool. He didn't need to go to all that trouble to put me in his debt so I'd side him. If he'd come and asked for my help, knowing how important Freddie believes this spur-line to be, I'd have given it to him."[1]

1. *Once again, Michael Meacher received more lenient treatment than he deserved. Taking him to Mulrooney, Dusty Fog told him to get his horse and make sure their paths never crossed again. However, despite having twice escaped a well deserved term of imprisonment in the Kansas State Penitentiary, he declined to turn over a new leaf and, becoming involved in a bank hold up which went wrong, he was killed along with the rest of the gang.*

1a. *As Dusty Fog hoped, the events brought about a reconciliation between Harland Todhunter Senior and his son. Taking over in place of Raymond Sangster, Junior was successful in laying the spur-line until it reached its destination in Canada. He was also involved in the negotia-*

tions for the use of the bridge over the Platte River and the right of way across the Beefhead ranch. During these negotiations he and Antonia Front de Boeuf became so attracted to one another, they were married on the day the construction was completed. Furthermore, with the work in such capable control, the small Texan was able to return to Mulrooney and spend a few days with his wife before setting out for the OD Connected ranch. However, prior to leaving the town, he and the other members of Ole Devil's floating outfit were involved in the events we recorded in: THE GENTLE GIANT.

Appendix One

Following his enrolment in the Army of the Confederate States,[1] by the time he reached the age of seventeen, Dustine Edward Marsden "Dusty" Fog had won promotion in the field to the rank of captain and was put in command of Company "C," Texas Light Cavalry.[2] At the head of them throughout the campaign in Arkansas, he had earned the reputation for being an exceptional military raider and a worthy contemporary of Turner Ashby and John Singleton "the Grey Ghost" Mosby, the South's other leading exponents of what would later become known as "commando" raids.[3] In addition to averting a scheme by a Union General to employ a virulent version of what was later to be given the name, "mustard gas" following its use by Germans in World War I[4] and preventing a pair of pro-Northern fanatics from starting an Indian uprising which would have decimated much of Texas,[5] he had supported Belle "the Rebel Spy" Boyd on two of her most dangerous assignments.[6]

At the conclusion of the War Between The States, Dusty became the *segundo* of the great OD Connected ranch—its brand being a letter O to which was attached a D—in Rio Hondo County, Texas. Its owner, and his maternal uncle, General Jackson Baines "Ole Devil" Hardin, C.S.A., had been crippled in a riding accident and was confined to a wheelchair.[7] This placed much responsibility, including the need to handle an important mission—with the future relationship between the United States and Mexico at stake—upon his young shoulders.[8] While carrying out the assignment, he met Mark

Counter and the Ysabel Kid. Not only did they do much to bring it to a successful conclusion, they became his closest friends and leading lights of the ranch's floating outfit.[9] After helping to gather horses to replenish the ranch's depleted remuda,[10] he was sent to assist Colonel Charles Goodnight[11] on the trail drive to Fort Sumner, New Mexico, which did much to help Texas recover from the impoverished conditions left by the War.[12] With that achieved, he had been equally successful in helping Goodnight convince other ranches it would be possible to drive large herds of longhorn cattle to the railroad in Kansas.[13]

Having proven himself to be a first class cowhand, Dusty went on to become acknowledged as a very competent trail boss,[14] roundup captain,[15] and town taming lawman.[16] Competing in the first Cochise County Fair in Arizona against a number of well known exponents of very rapid drawing and accurate shooting with revolvers, he won the title, "The Fastest Gun In The West."[17] In later years, following his marriage to Lady Winifred Amelia "Freddie Woods" Besgrove-Woodstole,[18] he became a noted diplomat.

Dusty never found his lack of stature an impediment to his achievements. In fact, he occasionally found it helped him to achieve a purpose.[19] To supplement his natural strength,[20] also perhaps with a desire to distract attention from his small size, he had taught himself to be completely ambidextrous.[21] Possessing perfectly attuned reflexes, he could draw either, or both, his Colts—whether the 1860 Army Model,[22] or their improved "descendant," the fabled 1873 Model "Peacemaker"[25]—with lightning speed and shoot most accurately. Furthermore, Ole Devil Hardin's "valet," Tommy Okasi, was Japanese and a trained *samurai* warrior.[24] From him, as was the case with the General's "granddaughter," Elizabeth "Betty" Hardin,[25] Dusty learned ju-jitsu and karate. Neither form of unarmed combat had received the publicity they would be given in later years and were little known in the Western Hemisphere at that time. Therefore, Dusty found the knowledge useful when he had to fight with bare hands against larger, heavier and stronger men.

1. Details of some of Dustine Edward Marsden "Dusty" Fog's activities prior to his enrolment are given in: *Part Five, "A Time For Improvisation, Mr. Blaze," J.T.'S HUNDREDTH*.

2. Told in: *YOU'RE IN COMMAND NOW, MR. FOG*.

3. Told in: *THE BIG GUN, UNDER THE STARS AND BARS, Part One, "The Futility of War," THE FASTEST GUN IN TEXAS* and *KILL DUSTY FOG!*

4. Told in: *A MATTER OF HONOUR*.

5. Told in: *THE DEVIL GUN*.

6. Told in: *THE COLT AND THE SABRE* and *THE REBEL SPY*.

6a. More details of the career of Belle "The Rebel Spy" Boyd can be found in: *MASTER OF TRIGGERNOMETRY; THE BLOODY BORDER; BACK TO THE BLOODY BORDER*—Berkley Books, New York, August, 1978 edition re-titled, *RENEGADE—THE HOODED RIDERS; THE BAD BUNCH SET; SET A-FOOT; TO ARMS! TO ARMS! IN DIXIE!; THE SOUTH WILL RISE AGAIN; THE QUEST FOR BOWIE'S BLADE; Part Eight, "Affair Of Honour," J.T.'S HUNDREDTH* and *Part Five, "The Butcher's Fiery End," J.T.'S LADIES*.

7. Told in: *Part Three, "The Paint," THE FASTEST GUN IN TEXAS*.

7a. Further information about the General's earlier career is given in the *Ole Devil Hardin* and *Civil War* series. His death is recorded in, *DOC LEROY, M.D.*

8. Told in: *THE YSABEL KID*.

9. *"Floating Outfit"*: a group of four to six cowhands employed by a large ranch to work the more distant sections of the property. Taking food in a chuck wagon, or "greasy sack" on the back of a mule, they would be away from the ranch house for long periods and so were selected for their honesty, loyalty, reliability, and capability in all aspects of their work. Because of General Hardin's prominence in the affairs of Texas, the OD Connected's floating outfit were frequently sent to assist such of his friends who found themselves in difficulties or endangered.

10. Told in: *.44 CALIBRE MAN* and *A HORSE CALLED MOGOLLON*.

11. Rancher and master cattleman Charles Goodnight never served in the Army. The rank was honorary and granted by his fellow Texans in respect for his abilities as a fighting man and leader.

11a. In addition to playing an active part in the events recorded in the books referred to in *Footnotes 13* and *14*, Colonel Goodnight makes "guest" appearances in: *Part One, "The Half Breed," THE HALF BREED;* it's "expansion," *WHITE INDIANS* and *IS-A-MAN*.

11b. Although Dusty Fog never received higher official rank than Captain, in the later years of his life, he too was given the honorific, "Colonel" for possessing the same qualities.

12. Told in: *GOODNIGHT'S DREAM*—Bantam Books, U.S.A., July 1974 edition re-titled, *THE FLOATING OUTFIT*, despite our already hav-

ing had a volume of that name published by Corgi Books, U.K., see *Footnote 19*—and *FROM HIDE AND HORN*.

13. Told in: *SET TEXAS BACK ON HER FEET*—although Berkley Books, New York re-titled their October, 1978 edition *VIRIDIAN'S TRAIL*, they reverted to the original when re-issuing the book in July, 1980—and *THE HIDE AND TALLOW MEN*.

14. Told in: *TRAIL BOSS*.

15. Told in: *THE MAN FROM TEXAS*.

16. Told in: *QUIET TOWN*; *THE MAKING OF A LAWMAN*; *THE TROUBLE BUSTERS*; *THE GENTLE GIANT*; *DECISION FOR DUSTY FOG*; *DIAMONDS, EMERALDS, CARDS AND COLTS*; *THE CODE OF DUSTY FOG*; *THE SMALL TEXAN* and *THE TOWN TAMERS*.

17. Told in: *GUN WIZARD*.

18. Lady Winifred Besgrove-Woodstole appears as "Freddie Woods' in: *THE TROUBLE BUSTERS*; *THE MAKING OF A LAWMAN*; *THE GENTLE GIANT*; *BUFFALO ARE COMING! THE FORTUNE HUNTERS*; *WHITE STALLION, RED MARE*; *THE WHIP AND THE WAR LANCE* and *Part Five, "The Butcher's Fiery End," J.T.'S LADIES*. She also "guest" stars under her married name, Mrs. Freddie Fog, in: *NO FINGER ON THE TRIGGER*.

19. Three occasions when Dusty Fog utilized his small size to his advantage are described in: *KILL DUSTY FOG!*; *Part One, "Dusty Fog And The Schoolteacher," THE HARD RIDERS*; its "expansion," *MASTER OF TRIGGERNOMETRY* and *Part One, "The Phantom of Gallup Creek," THE FLOATING OUTFIT*.

20. Two examples of how Dusty Fog exploited his exceptional physical strength are given in: *MASTER OF TRIGGERNOMETRY* and *THE PEACEMAKERS*.

21. The ambidextrous prowess was in part hereditary. It was possessed and exploited with equal success by Freddie and Dusty's grandson, Alvin Dustine "Cap" Fog who also inherited his grandfather's physique of a Hercules in miniature. Alvin utilized these traits to help him be acknowledged as one of the finest combat pistol shots in the United States during the Prohibition era and to earn his nickname by becoming the youngest man ever to hold rank of Captain in the Texas Rangers. See the *Alvin Dustine "Cap" Fog* series for further details of his career.

22. Although the military sometimes claimed derisively it was easier to kill a sailor than a soldier, the weight factor of the respective weapons had caused the United States' Navy to adopt a revolver of .36 calibre while the Army employed the larger .44. The reason was that the weapon would be carried on a seaman's belt and not—handguns having been originally and primarily developed for use by cavalry—on the person or saddle of a man who would be doing most of his travelling and fighting from the back of a horse. Therefore, .44 became known as the "Army" calibre and .36, the "Navy."

23. Details about the Colt Model P of 1873, more frequently known as "the Peacemaker" can be found in those volumes following *THE PEACE-MAKERS* in our list of *Floating Outfits* series' titles in chronological sequence.

24. *"Tommy Okasi"* is an Americanised corruption of the name given by the man in question, who had left Japan for reasons which the Hardin, Fog and Blaze families refuse to divulge even at this late date, when he was rescued from a derelict vessel in the China Sea by a ship under the command of General Hardin's father.

25. The members of the Hardin, Fog and Blaze families cannot—or *will not*—make any statement upon the exact relationship between Elizabeth "Betty" and her "grandfather," General Hardin.

25a. Betty Hardin appears in: *Part Five, "A Time for Improvisation, Mr. Blaze," J.T.'S HUNDREDTH; Part Four, "It's Our Turn to Improvise, Miss Blaze," J.T.'S LADIES; KILL DUSTY FOG!; THE BAD BUNCH; McGRAW's INHERITANCE; Part Two, "The Quartet," THE HALF BREED; THE RIO HONDO WAR* and *GUNSMOKE THUNDER*.

Appendix Two

With his exceptional good looks and magnificent physical development,[1] Mark Counter presented the kind of appearance many people expected of a man with the reputation gained by his *amigo*, Captain Dustine Edward Marsden "Dusty Fog." It was a fact of which they took advantage when the need arose.[2] On one occasion, it was also the cause of the blond giant being subjected to a murder attempt although the Rio Hondo gun wizard was the intended victim.[3]

While serving as a lieutenant under the command of General Bushrod Sheldon in the War Between the States, Mark's merits as an efficient and courageous officer had been overshadowed by his unconventional taste in uniforms. Always something of a dandy, coming from a wealthy family had allowed him to indulge in his whims. Despite considerable opposition and disapproval from hide-bound senior officers, his adoption of a "skirtless" tunic in particular had come to be much copied by the other rich young bloods of the Confederate States' Army.[4] Similarly in later years, having received an independent income through the will of a maiden aunt,[5] his taste in attire had dictated what the well dressed cowhand from Texas would wear to be in fashion.

When peace had come between the North and the South, Mark had accompanied Sheldon to fight for Emperor Maximilian in Mexico. There he had met Dusty Fog and the Ysabel Kid. On returning with them to Texas, he had received an offer to join the floating outfit of the OD Connected ranch. Knowing his two older brothers could help his father, Big Ranse, to run the family's R Over C ranch in the Big Bend country—and considering life would be more enjoyable and exciting in the company of his two *amigos*—he accepted.

An expert cowhand, Mark had become known as Dusty's right bower.[6] He had also gained acclaim by virtue of his enormous strength. Among other feats, it was told how he used a tree-trunk in the style of a Scottish caber to dislodge outlaws from a cabin in which they had forted up,[7] and broke the neck of a Texan longhorn steer with his bare hands.[8] He had acquired further fame for his ability at bare handed rough-house brawling. However, due to spending so much time in the company of the Rio Hondo gun wizard, his full potential as a gun fighter received little attention. Nevertheless, men who were competent to judge such matters stated that he was second only to the small Texan when it came to drawing fast and shooting accurately with a brace of long barrelled Colt revolvers.[9]

Many women found Mark irresistible, including Martha "Calamity Jane" Canary,[10] However in his younger days, only one—the lady outlaw, Belle Starr—held his heart.[11] It was not until several years after her death that he courted and married Dawn Sutherland, who he had first met on the trail drive taken by Colonel Charles Goodnight to Fort Sumner, New Mexico.[12] The discovery of oil on their ranch brought an added wealth to them and this commodity now forms the major part of the present members of the family's income.[13]

Recent biographical details we have received from the current head of the family, Andrew Mark "Big Andy" Counter, establish that Mark was descended on his mother's side from Sir Reginald Front de Boeuf, notorious as the lord of Torquilstone Castle in Medieval England[14] and who lived up to the family motto, *Cave Adsum*.[15] However, although a maternal aunt and her son, Jessica and Trudeau Front de Boeuf, behaved in a way which suggested they had done so,[16] the blond giant had not inherited the very unsavoury character and behaviour of his ancestor.

1. Two of Mark Counter's grandsons, Andrew Mark "Big Andy" Counter and Ranse Smith inherited his good looks and exceptional physique as did two great-grandsons, Deputy Sheriff Bradford "Brad" Counter and James

Allenvale "Bunduki" Gunn. Unfortunately, while willing to supply information about other members of his family, past and present, "Big Andy" has so far declined to allow publication of any of his own adventures.

1a. Some details of Ranse Smith's career as a peace officer during the Prohibition era are recorded in: *THE JUSTICE OF COMPANY "Z"* and *THE RETURN OF RAPIDO CLINT AND MR. J.G. REEDER*.

1b. Brad Counter's activities are described in: *Part Eleven, "Preventive Law Enforcement," J.T.'S HUNDREDTH* and the *Rockabye County* series, covering aspects of law enforcement in present day Texas.

1c. Some of James Gunn's life story is told in: *Part Twelve, "The Mchawi's Powers," J.T.'S HUNDREDTH* and the *Bunduki* series. His nickname arose from the Swahili word for a hand held firearm of any kind being, *"bunduki"* and gave rise to the horrible pun that when he was a child he was, *"Toto ya Bunduki,"* meaning, "Son of a Gun."

2. One occasion is recorded in: *THE SOUTH WILL RISE AGAIN*.

3. The incident is described in: *BEGUINAGE*.

4. The *Manual of Dress Regulations* for the Confederate States Army stipulated that the tunic should have "a skirt extending half way between hip and knee."

5. The legacy also caused two attempts to be made upon Mark's life, see: *CUT ONE, THEY ALL BLEED* and *Part Two, "We Hang Horse Thieves High," J.T.'S HUNDREDTH*.

6. "Right bower"; second in command, derived from the name given to the second highest trump card in the game of euchre.

7. Told in: *RANGELAND HERCULES*.

8. Told in: *THE MAN FROM TEXAS*, this is a rather "pin the tail on the donkey" title used by our first publishers to replace our own, *ROUNDUP CAPTAIN*, which we considered far more apt.

9. Evidence of Mark Counter's competence as a gun fighter and his standing compared to Dusty Fog is given in: *GUN WIZARD*.

10. Martha "Calamity Jane" Canary's meetings with Mark Counter are described in: *Part One, "The Bounty On Belle Starr's Scalp," TROUBLED RANGE*; its "expansion," *CALAMITY, MARK AND BELLE*; *Part One, "Better Than Calamity," THE WILDCATS*; its "expansion," *CUT ONE, THEY ALL BLEED*; *THE BAD BUNCH*; *THE FORTUNE HUNTERS*; *THE BIG HUNT* and *GUNS IN THE NIGHT*.

10a. Further details about the career of Martha Jane Canary are given in the *Calamity Jane* series, also; *Part Seven, "Deadwood, August the 2nd, 1876," J.T.'S HUNDREDTH*; *Part Six, "Mrs. Wild Bill," J.T.'S LADIES*, and she makes a "guest" appearance in, *Part Two, "A Wife For Dusty Fog," THE SMALL TEXAN*.

11. How Mark Counter's romance with Belle Starr commenced, progressed and ended is told in: *Part One, "The Bounty On Belle Starr's Scalp," TROUBLED RANGE*: its "expansion," *CALAMITY, MARK AND BELLE*; *THE BAD BUNCH*; *RANGELAND HERCULES*; *THE CODE OF*

DUSTY FOG; Part Two, "We Hang Horse Thieves High," J.T.'S HUN-DREDTH; THE GENTLE GIANT; Part four, "A Lady Known as Belle," THE HARD RIDERS and GUNS IN THE NIGHT.

11a. Belle Starr "stars"—no pun intended— in: *DIAMONDS, EMER-ALDS, CARDS AND COLTS; Part Five, "Another Kind of Badger Game," MORE J.T.'S LADIES* and *WANTED! BELLE STARR.*

11b. She also makes "guest" appearances in: *THE QUEST FOR BOWIE'S BLADE; Part one, "The Set-Up," SAGEBRUSH SLEUTH;* its "expansion," *WACO'S BADGE* and *Part Six, "Mrs. Wild Bill," J.T.'S LADIES.*

11c. We are frequently asked why it is the "Belle Starr" we describe is so different from a photograph which appears in various books. The researches of the world's foremost fictionist genealogist, Philip Jose Farmer—author of, amongst numerous other works, *TARZAN ALIVE, A Definitive Biography of Lord Greystoke* and *DOC SAVAGE, His Apocalyptic Life*—with whom we consulted have established the lady about whom we are writing is not the same person as another equally famous bearer of the name. However, the Counter family have asked Mr. Farmer and ourselves to keep her true identity a secret and this we intend to do.

12. Told in: *GOODNIGHT'S DREAM* and *FROM HIDE AND HORN.*

13. This is established by inference in: *Case Three, "The Deadly Ghost," YOU'RE A TEXAS RANGER, ALVIN FOG.*

14. See: *IVANHOE,* by Sir Walter Scott.

15. "Cave Adsum," roughly translated from Latin, "Beware, I Am Here."

16. Some information about Jessica and Trudeau Front de Boeuf can be found in: *CUT ONE, THEY ALL BLEED* and *Part Three, "Responsibility to Kinfolks," OLE DEVIL'S HANDS AND FEET.*

Appendix Three

Raven Head, only daughter of Chief Long Walker, war leader of the *Pehnane*—Wasp, Quick Stringer, Raider—Comanche's Dog Soldier lodge and his French Creole *pairaivo*,[1] married an Irish-Kentuckian adventurer, Big Sam Ysabel, but died giving birth to their first child.

Baptized "Loncey Dalton Ysabel," the boy was raised after the fashion of the *Nemenuh*.[2] With his father away from the camp for much of the time, engaged upon the family's combined businesses of mustanging—catching and breaking wild horses[3]—and smuggling, his education had largely been left in the hands of his maternal grandfather.[4] From Long Walker, he learned all those things a Comanche warrior must know: how to ride the wildest freshly caught mustang, or make a trained animal subservient to his will while "raiding"—a polite name for the favourite pastime of the male *Nemenuh*, stealing horses—to follow the faintest tracks and just as effectively conceal signs of his own passing;[5] to locate hidden enemies, or keep out of sight himself when the need arose; to move in silence on the darkest of nights, or through the thickest cover; to know the ways of wild creatures[6] and, in some cases, imitate their calls so well that others of their kind were fooled.[7]

The boy proved a most excellent pupil at all the subjects. Nor were practical means of protecting himself forgotten. Not only did he learn to use all the traditional weapons of the Comanche,[8] when he had come into the possession of firearms, he had inherited his father's Kentuckian skill at shooting with a rifle and, while not *real* fast on the draw—taking

171

slightly over a second to bring his Colt Second Model of 1848 Dragoon revolver and fire, whereas a tophand could practically halve that time—he could perform passably with it. Furthermore, he won his *Nemenuh* "man-name," *Cuchilo*, Spanish for "Knife," by his exceptional ability at wielding one. In fact, it was claimed by those best qualified to judge that he could equal the alleged designer in performing with the massive and special type of blade which bore the name of Colonel James Bowie.[9]

Joining his father in smuggling expeditions along the Rio Grande, the boy became known to the Mexicans of the border country as *Cabrito*—the Spanish name for a young goat—a nickname which arose out of hearing white men refer to him as the "Ysabel Kid," but it was spoken *very* respectfully in that context. Smuggling was not an occupation to attract the meek and mild of manner, yet even the roughest and toughest of the bloody border's denizens came to acknowledge it did not pay to rile up Big Sam Ysabel's son. The education received by the Kid had not been calculated to develop any over-inflated belief in the sanctity of human life. When crossed, he dealt with the situation like a *Pehnane* Dog Soldier—to which war lodge of savage and *most* efficient warriors he had earned initiation—swiftly and in an effectively deadly manner.

During the War Between The States, the Kid and his father had commenced by riding as scouts for Colonel John Singleton "the Grey Ghost" Mosby. Soon, however, their specialized knowledge and talents were diverted to having them collect and deliver to the Confederate States' authorities in Texas supplies which had been purchased in Mexico, or run through the blockade by the United States' Navy into Matamoros. It was hard and dangerous work,[10] but never more so than the two occasions when they became engaged in assignments with Belle "the Rebel Spy" Boyd.[11]

Soon after the War ended, Sam Ysabel was murdered. While hunting down the killers, the Kid met Captain Dustine Edward Marsden "Dusty" Fog and Mark Counter. When the mission upon which they were engaged was brought to its successful conclusion, learning the Kid no longer wished to go on either smuggling or mustanging, the small Texan offered him employment at the OD Connected ranch. It had been in the capacity as scout rather than ordinary cowhand that he was required and his talents in that field were frequently of the greatest use as a member of the floating outfit.

The acceptance of the job by the Kid was of the greatest benefit all around. Dusty acquired another loyal friend who was ready to stick to him through any kind of peril. The ranch obtained the services of an extremely capable and efficient fighting man. For his part, the Kid was turned from a life of petty crime—with the ever present danger of having his illicit activities develop into serious law breaking—and became a useful and law abiding member of society. Peace officers and honest citizens might have found cause to feel grateful for that. His *Nemenuh* upbringing would have made him a terrible and murderous outlaw if he had been driven into a life of violent crime.

Obtaining his first repeating rifle—a Winchester Model of 1866, although at first known as the "New Improved Henry," nicknamed the "Old Yellowboy" because of its brass frame— while in Mexico with Dusty and Mark, the Kid had soon become an expert in its use. At the First Cochise County Fair in Arizona, despite circumstances compelling him to use a weapon with which he was not familiar,[12] he won the first prize in the rifle shooting competition against stiff opposition. The prize was one of the legendary Winchester Model of 1873 rifles which qualified for the honoured designation, "One Of A Thousand."[13]

It was, in part, through the efforts of the Kid that the majority of the Comanche bands agreed to go on the reservation, following attempts to ruin the signing of the treaty.[14] It was to a large extent due to his efforts that the outlaw town of Hell was located and destroyed.[15] Aided by Annie "Is-A-Man" Singing Bear—a girl of mixed parentage who gained the distinction of becoming accepted as a *Nemenuh* warrior[16]—he played a major part in preventing the then attempted theft of Morton Lewis' ranch provoking trouble with the *Kwehareh-nuh* Comanche.[17] To help a young man out of difficulties caused by a gang of card cheats, he teamed up with the lady outlaw, Belle Starr.[18] When he accompanied Martha "Calamity Jane" Canary to inspect a ranch she had inherited, they became involved in as dangerous a situation as either had ever faced.[19]

Remaining at the OD Connected ranch until he, Dusty and Mark met their deaths whilst on a hunting trip to Kenya shortly after the turn of the century, his descendants continued to be associated with the Hardin, Fog and Blaze clan and the Counter family.[20]

1. "Pairaivo": first, or favourite wife. As is the case with the other Comanche terms, this is a phonetic spelling.
2. "Nemenuh": "the People," the Comanches' name for themselves and their nation. Members of other tribes with whom they came into contact called them, frequently with good cause, the *"Tshaoh,"* the "Enemy People."
3. A description of the way in which mustangs operated is given in: .44 CALIBRE MAN and *A HORSE CALLED MOGOLLON*.
4. Told in: *COMANCHE*.
5. An example of how the Ysabel Kid could conceal his tracks is given in: *Part One, "The Half Breed," THE HALF BREED*.
6. Two examples of how the Ysabel Kid's knowledge of wild animals was turned to good use are given in: *OLD MOCCASINS ON THE TRAIL* and *BUFFALO ARE COMING!*
7. An example of how well the Ysabel Kid could impersonate the call of a wild animal is recorded in: *Part Three, "A Wolf's A Knowing Critter," J.T.'S HUNDREDTH*.
8. One occasion when the Ysabel Kid employed his skill with traditional Comanche weapons is described in: *RIO GUNS*.
9. Some researchers claim that the actual designer of the knife which became permanently attached to Colonel James Bowie's name was his oldest brother, Rezin Pleasant. Although it is generally conceded the maker was James Black, a master cutler in Arkansas, some authorities state it was manufactured by Jesse Cliffe, a white blacksmith employed by the Bowie family on their plantation in Rapides Parish, Louisiana.
9a. What happened to James Bowie's knife after his death in the final assault of the siege of the Alamo Mission, San Antonio de Bexar, Texas, on March the 6th, 1836, is told in: *GET URREA* and *THE QUEST FOR BOWIE'S BLADE*.
9b. As all James Black's knives were custom made, there were variations in their dimensions. The specimen owned by the Ysabel Kid had a blade eleven and a half inches in length, two and a half inches wide and a quarter of an inch thick at the guard. According to William "Bo" Randall,

of Randall-Made Knives, Orlando, Florida—a master cutler and authority upon the subject in his own right—James Bowie's knife weighed forty-three ounces, having a blade eleven inches long, two and a quarter inches wide and three-eighths of an inch thick. His company's Model 12 "Smithsonian" bowie knife—one of which is owned by James Allenvale "Bunduki" Gunn, details of whose career can be found in the *Bunduki* series—is modelled on it.

9c. One thing all "bowie" knives have in common, regardless of dimensions, is a "clip" point. The otherwise unsharpened "back" of the blade joins and becomes an extension of the main cutting surface in a concave arc, whereas a "spear" point—which is less utilitarian—is formed by the two sides coming together in symmetrical curves.

10. An occasion when Big Sam Ysabel went on a mission without his son is recorded in: *THE DEVIL GUN*.

11. Told in: *THE BLOODY BORDER* and *BACK TO THE BLOODY BORDER*.

12. The circumstances are described in: *GUN WIZARD*.

13. When manufacturing the extremely popular Winchester Model of 1873 rifle—which they claimed to be the "Gun Which Won The West"—the makers selected all those barrels found to shoot with exceptional accuracy to be fitted with set triggers and given a special fine finish. Originally, these were inscribed, "1 of 1,000," but this was later changed to script, "One Of A Thousand." However, the title was a considerable understatement. Only one hundred and thirty-six out of a total production of 720,610 qualified for the distinction. Those of a grade lower were to be designated, "One Of A Hundred," but only seven were so named. The practice commenced in 1875 and was discontinued three years later because the management decided it was not good sales policy to suggest different grades of gun were being produced.

14. Told in: *SIDEWINDER*.

15. Told in: *HELL IN THE PALO DURO* and *GO BACK TO HELL*.

16. How Annie Singing Bear acquired the distinction of becoming a warrior and won her "man-name" is told in: *IS-A-MAN*.

17. Told in: *WHITE INDIANS*.

18. Told in: *Part Two, "The Poison And The Cure," WANTED! BELLE STARR*.

19. Told in: *WHITE STALLION, RED MARE*.

20. Mark Scrapton, a grandson of the Ysabel Kid, served as a member of Company "Z," Texas Rangers, with Alvin Dustine "Cap" Fog and Ranse Smith—respectively grandson of Captain Dustine Edward Marsden "Dusty" Fog and Mark Counter—during the Prohibition era. Information about their specialized duties is given in the *Alvin Dustine "Cap" Fog* series.

Appendix Four

Left an orphan almost from birth by an Indian raid and acquiring the only name he knew from the tribe involved,[1] Waco was raised as one of a North Texas rancher's large family.[2] Guns were always part of his life and his sixteenth birthday saw him riding with the tough, "wild onion" crew of Clay Allison. Like their employer, the CA cowhands were notorious for their wild and occasionally dangerous behaviour. Living in the company of such men, all older than himself, the youngster had become quick to take offense and well able, eager even, to prove he could draw his revolvers with lightning speed and shoot very accurately. It had seemed only a matter of time before one shootout too many would see him branded as a killer and fleeing from the law with a price on his head.

Fortunately for Waco and—as was the case with the Ysabel Kid—law abiding citizens, that day did not come!

From the moment Dusty Fog saved the youngster's life during a cattle stampede, at some considerable risk to his own, a change for the better had commenced.[3] Leaving Allison, with the blessing of the "Washita curly wolf," Waco had become a member of the OD Connected ranch's floating outfit. The other members of that elite group treated him like a favourite younger brother and taught him many useful lessons. Instruction in bare handed combat was provided by Mark Counter. The Kid showed him how to read tracks and other secrets of the scout's trade. From a friend who was a professional gambler, Frank Derringer,[4] had come information about the ways of honest and dishonest followers of his chosen field of endeavour. However, it was from the Rio Hondo gun wizard that the most important advice had come. *When* (he already knew well enough *how*) to shoot. Dusty had also supplied training which, helped by an inborn flair for deductive reasoning, turned him into a peace officer of exceptional merit. After serving in other official capacities,[5] then with the Arizona Rangers[6]—in the company of Marvin Eldridge "Doc" Leroy[7]—and as sheriff of Two Forks County, Utah,[8] he was eventually appointed a United States' marshal.[9]

1. Alvin Dustine "Cap" Fog informs us that at his marriage to Elizabeth "Beth" Morrow, Waco used the surname of his adoptive family, "Catlan."
2. How Waco repaid his obligation to the family which raised him is told in: *WACO'S DEBT*.
3. Told in: *TRIGGER FAST*.
4. Frank Derringer appears in: *QUIET TOWN*, *THE MAKING OF A LAWMAN*, *THE TROUBLE BUSTERS*, *THE GENTLE GIANT* and *COLD DECK*, *HOT LEAD*.
5. Told in: *THE MAKING OF A LAWMAN*; *THE TROUBLE BUSTERS*; *THE GENTLE GIANT*; *DECISION FOR DUSTY FOG*; *DIAMONDS, EMERALDS, CARDS AND COLTS*; Part Five, "The Hired Butcher," *THE HARD RIDERS*; Part Four, "A Tolerable Straight Shooting Gun," *THE FLOATING OUTFIT*; Part two, "The Invisible Winchester," *OLE DEVIL'S HANDS AND FEET*; *THE SMALL TEXAN* and *THE TOWN TAMERS*.
6. During the 1870s, the Governor of Arizona formed this particular law enforcement agency to cope with the threat of serious organized law breaking in his Territory. A similar decision was taken by a later Governor and the Arizona Rangers were brought back into being. Why it was considered necessary to appoint the first force, how it operated and was finally disbanded is recorded in the *Waco* series and *Part Six*, "Keep Good Temper Alive," *J.T.'S HUNDREDTH*.
7. At the period of this narration, although having acquired a reputation for knowledge in medical matters, Marvin Eldridge "Doc" Leroy had not yet been able to attain his ambition of following his father's footsteps by becoming a qualified doctor. How he did so is recorded in: *DOC LEROY, M.D.*
8. Told in: *THE DRIFTER*, which also describes how Waco first met Elizabeth "Beth" Morrow.
9. Told in: *HOUND DOG MAN*.

Appendix Five

Throughout the years we have been writing, we have frequently received letters asking for various terms we employ to be explained in greater detail. While we do not have the slightest objection to such correspondence and always reply, we have found it saves much time consuming repetition to include those most frequently requested in each new title. We ask our "old hands," who have seen these items many times in the past, to remember there are always "new chums" coming along who have not and to bear with us. J.T.E.

1. We strongly suspect the trend in movies and television series made since the mid-1950's, wherein all cowhands are portrayed as heavily bearded, long-haired and filthy arose less from a desire on the part of the production companies to create "realism" than because there were so few actors available—particularly to play "supporting" roles—who were short haired and clean shaven. Another factor was because the "liberal" elements who were starting to gain control over much of the media seem to obtain some form of "ego trip" from showing dirty conditions, filthy habits and unkempt appearances. In our extensive reference library, we cannot find even a dozen photographs of actual *cowhands*—as opposed to civilian scouts for the Army, old time mountain men, or gold prospectors—with long hair and bushy beards. In fact, our reading on the subject and conversations with friends living in the Western States of America have led us to the conclusion that the term "long hair" was one of opprobrium in the Old West and Prohibition eras just as it still tends to be today in cattle raising country.

2. We have occasionally received mail claiming that the throwing of knives was *never* carried out in serious combat. To those who consider this to be correct, we would point out that James Bowie was credited with doing so and killing an assailant fleeing from an abortive attempt to am-

bush and murder him; see: THE IRON MISTRESS by William Wellman.

2a. There is at least one occasion recorded as having happened in World War II. This happened during the close quarters fighting which occurred after the U.S. Navy's destroyer, *Borie*, rammed and was locked against the German submarine, *U-405*, during the Battle of the Atlantic. In addition to more conventional ways of fighting, an American sailor threw his sheath knife from the deck of his ship and killed a German on the casing of the submarine to prevent a gun being manned; see Chapter 7, "Scratch One Pig Boat . . . Am Searching For More," THE SEA HUNTERS, by Kenneth Poolman and, Chapter Twelve, "An Epic Duel," AUTUMN OF THE U-BOATS, by Geoffrey Jones.

3. Although the military sometimes claimed it was easier to kill a sailor than a soldier, perhaps tongue in cheek, the weight factor of the respective weapons had been responsible for the decision by the United States' Navy to adopt a revolver with a calibre of .36 while the Army employed the heavier .44. The weapon would be carried upon the person of a seaman and not—handguns having been originally and primarily developed for single-handed use by cavalry—on the person or saddle of a soldier who would be doing much of his travelling and fighting from the back of a horse. Therefore, .44 became known as the "Army" and .36 as the "Navy" calibre.

4. We consider at best specious—at worst, a snobbish attempt to "put down" the myth and legends of the Old West—the frequently repeated assertion that the gun fighters of that era could not "hit a barn door at twenty yards." While willing to concede that the average person then, as now, would not have much skill in using a handgun, knowing his life would depend upon it, the professional *pistolero* on either side of the law expended time, money and effort to acquire proficiency. Furthermore, such a man did not carry a revolver to indulge in shooting at *anything* except at close range. He employed it as a readily accessible *weapon* which would incapacitate an enemy, preferably with the first shot, at close quarters, hence the preference for a cartridge of heavy calibre.

4a. With the exception of .22 calibre handguns intended for casual pleasure shooting, those specially designed for Olympic style "pistol" matches, the Remington XP100—one of which makes an appearance in: Case Two, "A Voice From The Past," THE LAWMEN OF ROCKABYE COUNTY—designed for "varmint" hunting at long distances, or medium to heavy calibre automatic pistols "accurized" and in the hands of a proficient exponent of modern "combat" shooting, a handgun is a short range *defensive* and not an *offensive* weapon. Any Old West gun fighter, or peace officer in the Prohibition era and present times, expecting to have to shoot at distances beyond about twenty *feet* would take the precaution of arming himself with a shotgun or a rifle.

5. "Make wolf bait," one term meaning to kill. Derived from the practice in the Old West, when a range was infested by stock killing predators—

not necessarily just wolves, but coyotes, the occasional jaguar in southern regions, black and grizzly bears—of slaughtering an animal and, having poisoned the carcase, leaving it to be devoured by the carnivores.

6. "Lance carrier." Because the war lance had such a high and special "medicine" significance, when a Comanche warrior elected to carry one, he was expected to be the first into battle and the last to leave the field no matter how adversely the fighting might be going for his band. However, providing he had discharged this responsibility honourably—and survived—he could decide to stop being a "lance carrier" whenever he wished without detriment to his reputation.

7. "Up to the Green River": to kill, generally with a knife. First produced on the Green River, at Greenfield, Massachusetts, in 1834, a very popular type of general purpose knife had the inscription, "*J. Russell & Co./Green River Works*" on the blade just below the hilt. Therefore any edged weapon thrust into an enemy "up to the Green River" would prove fatal whether it bore the inscription or not.

8. "Light a shuck," a cowhand term for leaving hurriedly. Derived from the habit in night camps on "open range" roundups and trail drives of supplying "shucks"—dried corn cobs—to be lit and used for illumination by anybody who had to leave the campfire and walk about in the darkness. As the "shuck" burned away very quickly, a person needed to hurry if wanting to benefit from its illumination.

9. The sharp toes and high heels of boots worn by cowhands were functional rather than merely decorative. The former could find and enter, or be slipped free from, a stirrup iron very quickly in an emergency. Not only did the latter offer a firmer brace against the stirrups, they could be spiked into the ground to supply added holding power when roping on foot.

10. Americans in general used the word, "cinch," derived from the Spanish, "cincha," to describe the short band made from coarsely woven horse hair, canvas, or cordage and terminated at each end with a metal ring which—together with the *latigo*—is used to fasten the saddle on the back of a horse. However, because of the word's connections with Mexico, Texans tended to employ the term, "girth," usually pronouncing it as "girt." As cowhands from the Lone Star State fastened the end of the lariat to the saddlehorn, even when roping half wild longhorn cattle or free-ranging mustangs, instead of relying upon a "dally" which could be slipped free almost instantaneously in an emergency, their rigs had double girths.

11. "Chaps": leather overalls worn by American cowhands as protection for the legs. The word, pronounced, "shaps," is an abbreviation of the Spanish, "*chaperejos*," or "*chaparreras*," meaning "leather breeches." Contrary to what is frequently shown in Western movies, no cowhand ever kept his chaps on when their protection was not required. Even if he should arrive in a town with them on, he would remove and either hang

them over his saddle, or leave them behind the bar in his favourite saloon for safe keeping until his visit was over.

12. "Hackamore": an Americanised corruption of the Spanish word, "*jaquima*," meaning "headstall." Very popular with Indians in particular, it was an ordinary halter, except for having reins instead of a leading rope. It had a headpiece something like a conventional bridle, a brow band about three inches wide which could be slid down the cheeks to cover the horse's eyes, but no throat latch. Instead of a bit, a "*bosal*"—a leather, rawhide, or metal ring around the head immediately above the mouth— was used as a means of control and guidance.

14. "Right as the Indian side of a horse"; absolutely correct. Derived from the habit of Indians mounting from the right, or "off" and not the left, or "near" side as was done by people of European descent and Mexicans.

15. "Mason-Dixon line," erroneously called the "Mason-Dixie line." The boundary between Pennsylvania and Maryland, as surveyed from 1763-67 by the Englishmen, Charles Mason and Jeremiah Dixon. It became considered as the dividing line separating the Southern "Slave" and Northern "Free" States.

16. "New England": the North East section of the United States—including Massachusetts, New Hampshire, Connecticut, Maine, Vermont and Rhode Island—which was first settled by people primarily from the British Isles.

17. "Gone to Texas": on the run from the law. During the white colonization period, which had commenced in the early 1820's, many fugitives from justice in America had fled to Texas and would continue to do so until annexation by the United States on February the 16th, 1846. Until the latter became a fact, they had known there was little danger of being arrested and extradited by the local authorities. In fact, like Kenya Colony from the 1920's to the outbreak of World War II—in spite of the number of honest, hard working and law abiding settlers genuinely seeking to make a permanent home there—Texas had gained a reputation for being a "place in the sun for shady people."

18. "Summer name": an alias. In the Old West, the only acceptable way to express doubt about the identity which was supplied when being introduced to a stranger was to ask, "Is that your *summer* name?"

19. In the Old West, the jurisdictional powers of various types of law enforcement agencies were established as follows. A town Marshal, sometimes called "constable" in smaller communities, and his deputies were confined to the town or city which hired them. A sheriff—who was generally elected into office for a set period of time—and his deputies were restricted to their own county. However, in less heavily populated areas, he might also serve as Marshal of the county seat. Texas and Arizona Rangers could go anywhere within the boundaries of their respective States, but technically were required to await an invitation from the local peace officers before participating in an investigation. Although a United

States Marshal and Deputy U.S. Marshal had jurisdiction everywhere throughout the country, their main function was the investigation of "Federal" crimes. Information about the organization and duties of a modern day Texas sheriff's office can be found in the *Rockabye County* series.

19a. As we explain in our *Alvin Dustine "Cap" Fog* series, by a special dispensation of the Governor during the Prohibition era, Company "Z" of the Texas Rangers was allowed to initiate operations without requesting permission under certain circumstances. During the late 1870's, the Governor of Arizona formed a similar force to cope with law breaking in his State. A similar decision was taken by a later Governor and the Arizona Rangers were brought back into being. Why it was considered necessary to organize the first force, how it operated and was finally disbanded is recorded in the *Waco* series and Part Four, "Keep Good Temper Alive," J.T.'S HUNDREDTH.

20. "Burro": in this context, a small wooden structure like the roof of a house upon which a saddle would be rested when not in use. Being so dependant upon his rig, a cowhand preferred to use a burro when one was available instead of laying it down or hanging it by a stirrup.

20a. Despite the misconception created by Western movies—even the late and great John Wayne being an offender—a cowhand would *never* toss down his saddle on its skirts. If no burro was available, he would either lay it on its side, or stand it on its head, somewhere it would be safely clear of anybody inadvertently stepping upon it.

THE END